MW01106311

KUSH
HOUᴙ

Volume I • Sin

RUSH

HOUЯ

A Journal of Contemporary Voices

MICHAEL CART, editor

DELACORTE PRESS

Published by Delacorte Press
an imprint of Random House Children's Books
a division of Random House, Inc., New York

Introduction copyright © 2004 by Michael Cart
"Sinphony" copyright © 2004 by Martin Matje
"A Life of Crime" copyright © 2004 by Brock Cole
"Smoke" copyright © 2004 by Joan Bauer
"One Size Fits All" and "Portrait of a Liar" copyright © 2004 by Nikki Grimes
"Good Deed" copyright © 2004 by Emma Donoghue
"The Sins of Salem" copyright © 2004 by Marc Aronson
Excerpt from *Leatherstone,* an unpublished novel, copyright © 2004
      by David Pabian
"Pages of Persecution" copyright © 2004 by Mark Podwal
"What Would I Have Done?" copyright © 2004 by Hazel Rochman
"Blood Knot" copyright © 2004 by Tom Feelings
"The Silk Ball" copyright © 2004 by Terry Davis
"Massage" copyright © 2004 by Sonya Sones
Excerpt from *Gone Lonesome,* an unpublished novel, copyright © 2004
      by Gary Miller
"Terror" copyright © 2004 by R. Gregory Christie
"The Terror Class" copyright © 2004 by Elizabeth Lorde-Rollins
"Intrinsic Value" copyright © 2004 by Alex Flinn
"Unfortunately Magnificent" copyright © 2004 by Chris Lynch, from the
      forthcoming novel *Inexcusable,* to be published by Atheneum Books
      for Young Readers
"Museum Piece" copyright © 2004 by Ron Koertge

Editorial advisory board: Frances Bradburn, Betty Carter, Aidan Chambers,
Pam Spencer Holley, Jennifer Hubert, George Nicholson, Joel Shoemaker, and
Deborah D. Taylor

Visit us on the Web! www.randomhouse.com/teens

Educators and librarians, for a variety of teaching tools, visit us at
www.randomhouse.com/teachers
ISBN: 0-385-73031-4 (trade)
ISBN: 0-385-90166-6 (lib. bdg.)
ISSN: 1547-0601

The text of this book is set in 12-point Adobe Garamond.
Book design by Vikki Sheatsley

Printed in the United States of America
April 2004   10 9 8 7 6 5 4 3 2 1   BVG

Contents

Introduction

Welcome to the first issue of *Rush Hour,* something new in publishing. Neither a magazine nor a book, we're the best of both: a cutting-edge literary journal of contemporary voices that will be published twice each year. Our contents are intended to be at once artful and risk-taking, innovative and—always—eclectic. In this inaugural issue, for example, you'll find original art, stories, essays, poetry, and excerpts from forthcoming novels. Though varied in form, each entry deals with a common theme: "Sin."

So why "Sin"? Well, for starters, each issue of *Rush Hour* will feature a theme that invites contributors to examine, in fresh and original ways, issues that affect the lives of today's readers. Among those chosen for future issues are "Bad Boys," "Face," and "Reckless." Like "Sin," each is intended to be open-ended, provocative, and thought-provoking. Of them all, however, "Sin" seems the most immediately relevant to a world ridden by guilt and riven by conflict that, though sometimes secular, more often seems rooted in religious belief—and disbelief. Just like sin. Simply say the word and many people immediately think of the Ten Commandments or the proverbial seven deadly sins—pride, covetousness, lust, anger, gluttony, envy, and sloth.

First posited by St. Gregory the Great, pope from 590 to 604, the seven deadly sins have inspired generations of authors and artists ever since—creative talents like Chaucer, Dante, Marlowe, Hieronymous Bosch, and too many others to list here. Suffice it to say, the topic of the seven deadly sins is still a hot one today. It recently inspired the hit movie *Seven,* starring Brad Pitt and Morgan Freeman, while a Google search results in no fewer than 55,000 entries! Clearly, sin is still much on our minds. But is it always deadly? Is it always deliberate? Is it always religious or is it sometimes secular? Who's to say what is sinful and what is not? And where will you find sin?

These are some of the questions that have inspired our contributors. Consider the following: Artist Martin Matje sets the stage with "Sinphony," his amusing cartoon about the wages of sin—and confession. Repression—not confession—is the order of the day in Brock Cole's darkly comic story about the everyday sins of self-denial and self-delusion. Sin, it seems, is everywhere. Joan Bauer finds it in a high-powered, truth-manipulating New York ad agency. Poet Nikki Grimes also finds sin in untruth, what she calls murder by mouth, which defined the life of the Biblical patriarch Jacob. Like Grimes, Emma Donoghue finds inspiration in a Bible story—that of the good Samaritan—as she reminds us, in her contemporary reimagining, that there are sins not only of commission but also of omission.

Marc Aronson finds our subject in the witchcraft trials of Salem, where "sin after sin after sin [was] kept spinning along by lies." Meanwhile, if the witches of Salem were doing the work of the Devil, as some alleged, so, perhaps, is the young protagonist of David Pabian's *Leatherstone,* a modern reimagining of the classic story of Frankenstein with its human usurpation of the power of creation.

In her thoughtful examination of the literature of the Holocaust, Hazel Rochman writes not about the creation of life but about its destruction by the unimaginably horrible sin of genocide. In an original drawing that accompanies this essay, Mark Podwal provides his own stunning visual interpretation of the catastrophic event.

Yet another aspect of man's inhumanity to man is provided by artist Tom Feelings in his haunting visual evocation of slavery in America. The inhumanity and wanton destructiveness of war are the subjects of Terry Davis's haunting story of America's covert military presence in the Cambodia of the 1970s.

Closer to the home of contemporary teenage life, Sonya Sones writes about the desire for sexual expression—and its frustration—that plagues the protagonist of her suite of poems, "Massage."

Are there unforgivable sins? Some would say that suicide is such a one. Read Gary Miller's powerful and haunting story, "Gone Lonesome," and decide for yourself.

Suicide by hanging turns to murder by lynching in artist R. Gregory Christie's wrenching image, ripped from America's terror-ridden past. Poet Elizabeth Lorde-Rollins finds a similar kind of terror prevailing in contemporary urban classrooms.

Similarly, emotional and physical violence fills the schoolrooms and playing fields that are the settings of Alex Flinn's and Chris Lynch's stories "Intrinsic Value" and "Unfortunately Magnificent."

Finally, poet Ron Koertge brings us full circle, back to the same wryly amused view of sin offered in Martin Matje's "Sinphony." But the pictures that Koertge writes about are ones that move; they're the flickering frames of a stag film that leave a teenage viewer breathless with disbelief.

So there you have it. The contents of our inaugural issue. Everything you always wanted to know about sin—and then some. Many of the names here are familiar—among them Terry Davis, Joan Bauer, Chris Lynch, and Brock Cole. But we're proud that some of these contemporary voices belong to previously unpublished writers, since discovering new talent and sharing it with you are an important part of *Rush Hour*'s reason for being, as is the opportunity to bring to you voices, both new and familiar, from other English-speaking countries. Young adult literature is now a global phenomenon, and *Rush Hour* will reflect that.

Look for more of all of this in our next issue, in which our contributors will explore another intriguing topic, "Bad Boys." Until then, welcome again to *Rush Hour*.

                                                    —Michael Cart, Editor

Sinphony

MARTIN MATJE

A Life of Crime

BROCK COLE

Gladys Durstweiller was standing in front of Teeter's Collectibles on Elmwood Avenue putting on her gloves when, without any warning, a scrawny woman in red glasses burst out of the store and accused her of shoplifting. It was so horrible, Gladys could hardly believe it was happening. She wouldn't have gone in the store except that she wanted to avoid a drunk who looked as if he might be going to talk to her. Inside, she'd asked about bus schedules and then looked at a collection of glass-and-silver perfume bottles on top of an old dresser just to be polite. Now this!

"Excuse me?" she said. As if she hadn't understood a word. "I think there's been some mistake." She appealed to the man who'd followed the scrawny woman out onto the street. He had a bow tie and wavy gray hair.

"I don't think so, miss," he said. "Let's not make a fuss." He squinted at the rooftops across the street as if he was getting signals from somebody up there.

"I'm afraid I don't have the faintest idea what you are talking about. Now, if you don't mind..."

"Mavis?" said the man to the scrawny woman. "Better call the police."

Gladys decided to run, but something was wrong with her legs. When she took a step, her foot seemed to go right through the pavement, and she sagged against the man's chest.

"Oh God, I didn't mean to," Gladys heard herself cry. "It was an accident!"

"Get her inside," said the man.

"No, no, no!" Gladys cried, and tried to fall in a heap on the ground. The man caught her under her arms. She could feel her blouse pull out of her waistband. A shoe came off, her jacket slid up over her head. She could smell her own smell, wild and terrified. Between them, the man and woman dragged her into the shop. She heard the door slam.

"Please," she cried. "Please don't hurt me!"

"Shut up!" said the man, pushing her down in a chair. "No one's going to hurt you." He stepped back and adjusted his tie. His hair was mussed. She could see a smear of what must have been her own lipstick on his shirtfront. It would probably never come out. The man fished the perfume bottle—it was little and squat with a silver filigree around the neck—out of her pocket and showed it to her.

"This is a very serious matter," he said, and she burst into tears. She knew it was serious. She hadn't before. It hadn't seemed real. Not the perfume bottle. Not the store. Not the man with his wavy hair and the woman in the red glasses. They had all seemed parts of a dream.

"I'm-sorry-I'm-sorry-I'm-sorry I don't know what's the matter with me. I never stole anything before; I don't know what I was thinking," she cried.

"It was a stupid, stupid thing to do. You should know better. You want me to call the police? Is that what you want?" The man waved the perfume bottle about as if he might smash it down on her head.

"No, no. Please, please don't. Ohgodohgodohgod..."

"How old are you? Do you live at home? I'm going to call your father."

"Oh God, no, don't do that. He'll kill me. He really will. He beats on me all the time...." She listened in horror to the stories she was telling. Another father, not her own, took shape before her eyes. Small, dirty, smelling of drink. "He joined AA but that didn't make things any better. I don't understand. It was supposed to make him good, wasn't it?"

"No. Only sober," said the man. He seemed amused now, and Gladys felt her spirits rise. She told them awful things. That she'd been abused in Sunday school by the teacher, and that she'd had two abortions. All lies. The woman in the red glasses gave her a cup of tea and a box of Kleenex. When they let her go, the man asked her if she was going to steal again.

"Oh, no. I never will. I promise."

"You've been lucky this time. You know that, don't you?"

"Yes, I know it. I really do."

"All right, then..."

At the door Gladys felt all the muscles in her spine go absolutely rigid. She didn't want to go home, she realized.

"Can I come back?" she asked. "I mean sometime?"

"No. Never ever," said the man, and pushed her out into the sunshine.

When she got home, she cried her eyes out. Her mom and dad were at work, so she had the house to herself. It smelled of floor wax and Pine-Sol. The whole first floor was done in linoleum that showed every footprint. Her mother could tell at a glance if there'd been a burglar before she actually stepped inside.

Gladys didn't even check to see if they'd been burgled. She threw her jacket and bag on the couch, ran upstairs, and flung herself on her bed. She cried for the following reasons: She was ashamed of stealing, ashamed of having gotten caught, and of having lied about having a terrible home life. She was crying, too, because she was a little bit in love with the man who ran the antique store, and now she could never see him again.

What did it matter anyway? She was a married woman, Mrs. Joe Bob Durstweiller, and that was something else she was crying about. She was a nineteen-year-old married woman. She'd met Joe Bob at the Rainbow Rink where she'd gone to learn how to roller-skate. He'd insisted on giving her all sorts of advice, and she had appreciated his being there at her side the first couple of times around the oval wooden floor. He had held her hand tightly in his. His free hand had rested lightly in the small of her back. The fingers sitting there on the little shelf where her spine started to curve out had made her so tense that she'd soon had a backache. Still, those couple of trips around the rink had given him a hold on her that she hadn't been able to shake. Before she knew it, she was married and Joe Bob was going around telling everyone he was the one who taught her how to roller-skate. It wasn't even true! She'd really taught herself just like everybody else. She didn't want to be married, either, as she found out almost at once. She and Joe Bob had been separated six months. It had turned out that he was crazy. He was a sex maniac. Those were exactly the words her mother had used after Gladys had told her about the goings-on in that little tract house Joe Bob had taken her to out in Clarence.

"A definite sex fiend," Mrs. Posner added, taking her daughter's hands and squeezing them. They were sitting up in her bedroom. It had been preserved just as it was the day she got married. Even the wadded-up Kleenex in the wastebasket was protected by a plastic Ziploc bag. It was all stained with makeup and tears. It made Gladys want to sob just to look at it. Oh lost innocence of youth! she thought. And she hadn't even told her mother the worst of it. Not about the vegetables. She'd watched him out in that patch of garden from the kitchen window and never had the faintest inkling of what he was planning to do with that Italian eggplant. She'd never be able to go in a produce section of a supermarket again without getting the cold sweats. And of course there were the photographs. Often

with the vegetables. She simply tried to block those from
her mind.

"I can't go back, Mama," she cried. "There's just no
way in the world I can go back."

"Don't even think about it," said Mrs. Posner. "It's
right out of the question. You'll stay right here, just like
the old times." She made Gladys put on one of her old
nightgowns still preserved in a plastic wardrobe with all of
her other high school clothes.

"You get in bed, and I'll go make some soup in the
microwave," she said, but Gladys was so upset she couldn't
bring herself to assume a prone position. It brought back
too many horrifying memories. She simply stood in the
closet and fingered the skirt of her old Camp Fire Girls
uniform. Was there any way in the world she could have
known what Joe Bob was going to turn out to be? She had
been searching her mind over and over again since almost
the first day. Sometimes when she was talking to him, he
had drawn himself up straight and leaned over as if he
weighed more on one side than the other. That was pretty
strange, come to think of it. When he did it, he would get
this funny look on his face, as if he was thinking about
something not very nice while she was trying to be pleasant about the wedding arrangements. And once he had
used the facilities under the stairs in the hall in such a
careless way that she'd been able to hear what was happening. She'd been in the kitchen about to make them both
banana smoothies when it had happened. She'd turned on
the blender quick as a wink, but still she was upset. Now

she couldn't even think about a banana smoothie without hearing all that splashing noise in her head. She should have known then what Joe Bob was going to turn out to be like, but how could she? She set her teeth and told herself that she had been forced to assume that he didn't realize how the sound would carry. It would take a mind as dirty as his to think otherwise.

Mrs. Posner had taken her father aside and explained how things stood when he'd come home from work that afternoon. From her bedroom, under the sheets now, Gladys could hear the murmur of their voices in the kitchen, and then the buzzer that meant the microwave had completed yet another task. A warm smell of cinnamon floated up the stairs. Gladys didn't think she could stand it. What was her future going to be like? Her throat began to close up, just as it had when she'd been exposed to cats as a child. She could feel hives start out under her chin.

Her father brought a plate of sticky buns upstairs and told her that he would try to arrange to have the marriage annulled. He wouldn't look at her. He was a big, shambling man whose head almost brushed the ceiling of the room as it sloped down toward the windows. Gladys could tell he'd never feel the way he used to about her. She'd never again be his little girl. Not after the things she'd submitted to. He would forgive her. Well, it wasn't her fault after all, but it was evident he would never feel the same. She was damaged goods. What an awful thought that was! She'd never realized what it meant before. Innocent of any crime, but damaged beyond repair.

"Was there ever any actual penetration?" her father asked, peering into the wastebasket with its treasure of childhood memories.

"Oh, take it away, take it away!" Gladys cried.

Her father straightened up, befuddled, knocking over the plate of sticky buns on her bedside table.

"I can't stand that smell of cinnamon," she explained. "I think I'm allergic."

Her father had never heard of someone developing an allergy as an adult. "Just out of the blue, so to speak," but when they took her to the doctor for a "complete physical," the doctor said it happened all the time. "Probably triggered in this case by emotional trauma." He had examined Gladys from head to toe without finding much wrong with her. He wouldn't speculate about the extent of her sexual experience, and seemed to regard it as a peculiar question. For the allergy, he prescribed an antihistamine and said she should stay away from sticky buns. Sticky buns and cinnamon toast, apple pie, elephant ears, bear claws, carrot cake, spice cake, spice drops, spice cookies, oatmeal raisin cookies, eggnog... It felt to Gladys as if her whole life was collapsing around her.

Things got worse. Joe Bob Durstweiller refused absolutely to give her a divorce. He drove over from Clarence to her parents' house in his blue Chevy Lumina and stood on the front steps leaning to one side.

"Get dressed, Gladys, and come home. You are my wife," he said.

Mr. Posner got out his shotgun that he used for quail hunting in the fall and told Joe Bob to leave.

"This is Gladys's home and always will be. Now get off my porch and don't come back." He felt fairly comfortable saying this, because, as he explained later to Gladys and her mother, that man in Alabama who had shot the Japanese exchange student for failing to freeze when instructed to do so had recently been acquitted. Gladys didn't understand at first.

"Joe Bob isn't Japanese," she said.

"Doesn't matter," said her father.

"You mean that you could shoot Joe Bob if he didn't freeze when you told him to?"

"In these circumstances," said her father.

This was a revelation. To think that an American could be shot, too. Gladys could hardly believe it. She wasn't sure she wanted Joe Bob shot, anyway. Some of the things he had done to her hadn't been all that unpleasant if she steeled herself to it.

When Joe Bob was gone, Mrs. Posner said that what they all needed was a cup of decaf. Gladys sat in her old place at the formica table in the kitchen while her father and mother made coffee and warmed up a Sara Lee pound cake. They were both big people, but they maneuvered around each other in the tiny kitchen in perfect harmony, as if they were performing the steps of a dance. Gladys looked around breathlessly, taking in the dear, familiar room. It was just as it was when she had left it, crisp and glistening with cleanliness. The old-fashioned freestanding stove and refrigerator. The sunburst clock on the wall. The jar where her mother kept the wooden spoons, shaped like a fat chicken.

"I feel like this is where I belong," said Gladys doubt-fully.

"I know what," said her mother, turning from the window with her soft little hand on her hip. "Let's just pretend this whole thing never happened. Let's just go back to the way things were before that man ever showed up."

Gladys looked to see if her father was going to agree, but he acted as if he hadn't even heard what his wife was saying. He was slicing up the pound cake, his brow furrowed, the yellow cake falling away from the black-handled knife in perfectly even slices.

"What if he comes back? Joe Bob, I mean," Gladys asked.

"We'll cross that bridge when we come to it," said her father.

"Oh, he won't bother us anymore," said Mrs. Posner, getting out the half-and-half. Neither she nor her husband had any patience with the people who were always trying to get them to use nondairy creamer or skim in their coffee. "Everything's going to be perfect. Just the way it used to be."

For a while it seemed to Gladys as if her mother might be going to be right. Joe Bob stopped calling. When the Posners' lawyer went to deliver the divorce papers, he reported back that the house in Clarence seemed to be shut up. He went to Joe Bob's place of work at A & E Autobody and was told that Mr. Durstweiller had quit and gone to Florida. There was no forwarding address.

Mr. Posner was disturbed by this news. First of all, he wanted to know exactly where Joe Bob was at any particular moment, and secondly he was concerned about a number of things that Gladys had left in the tract house when she had fled without her keys. Things that were hers beyond any question of law. It seemed outrageous to him that Joe Bob should simply have locked them up beyond reach and gone to Fort Lauderdale.

"You don't know he's in Fort Lauderdale," said Gladys. "You don't even know he's in Florida. That's just what someone said." She had a vision of Joe Bob cavorting on the beaches with almost-naked college students. A girl at church had told her it was common practice for these students to rent a motel room for one or two people and then to crowd in a dozen or more.

Her father gave her a dark look. "He might be anywhere," he said. "He might be in South America. I hope he *is* in South America. I don't want him around here. In the woods or someplace." He frowned darkly out the picture window past the bird feeder to the back of the property where a dark wood began. Gladys's heart turned over. The woods were the worst kind, full of spindly trees and black, spiky shadows. There was rumored to be a herd of deer there, which would come out at night and prowl through people's gardens. Oh God, she thought. Don't let him be there. Not with all those animals.

Her father got out a piece of paper and wrote at the top: "Property of Gladys Durstweiller (née Posner) currently at 133 Deer Creek Road, Clarence, New York."

"What's this?" she asked.

"Never mind. You just fill that out. Everything you left over there."

"Everything?" She thought of the underwear from Victoria's Secret in the top drawer of her dresser. The teddies and lacy bras, the thong bikinis and those bodysuits with those awful snaps right at her privates.

She refused to have anything to do with the list. "Besides, I don't think it makes sense. What do you mean, 'Property *at* 133 Deer Creek Road?' Shouldn't that be 'residing *at*' or 'deposited *at*'? Just 'property *at*' sounds awfully bald to me."

Her father was crushed by her talking back that way. He shrank down in his chair and looked away.

"Oh, Daddy, I'm sorry," Gladys told him. "I'll fill out the list right away. Soon as I can get a moment." Didn't she, she reminded herself, already have a million things to do? All those new clothes she and her mother had bought at the Prime Outlets in Niagara Falls had to be altered. She had normal length arms and legs and not those spidery limbs like the girls in the magazines. It was going to take hours.

She was working again, too. She had her old job back on the lunch shift at the Dew Drop Inn. It fell vacant just as she was making inquiries. "If that doesn't show that God works in mysterious ways," her mother said, "I don't know what does. It is such a relief to have things getting back to normal."

Were things getting back to normal? Was everything going to go on just like it used to? Gladys would lie in her bed at night and wonder. It certainly seemed as if she had slipped into her old routines, her old ways, almost without a hitch. She and her parents got up every morning at seven to get ready for work. They fell easily into the habits they had once had. It was her job, for example, to get the coffee machine ready in the evening before they went to bed so that her father just had to push the button when he came down in the morning.

"It's such a relief to have you back," he said one morning. This was after they'd made up over the tiff about the list of Property *abandoned* at 133 Deer Creek Road. "I don't know how often I've come down and pushed the button and nothing happened."

That must have been discouraging, Gladys thought. They really were glad to have her back. At work, too, everything seemed pretty much the same. There were some new faces. A Mexican working in the kitchen she hadn't seen before, and Ginger had hired a young man who was gay to take care of the salad bar. It was a responsible position, but she wouldn't let him go even after she found out.

"We all have to live with our mistakes," she said. Gladys felt offended for a moment, thinking that Ginger was perhaps thinking about Joe Bob, but then she gave herself a shake and reminded herself that people couldn't always tailor their every remark to her feelings.

On Sundays Gladys and her parents went to church. They attended the First Baptist on Military Road usually. It was where she and Joe Bob had been married. After the rehearsal, the minister had taken them aside for some counseling. He wanted them to understand how serious the step they were taking was, and read the passage from Saint Paul's letter to the Ephesians which explained that as

God was to man, so a husband was to his wife. As they were leaving, he slipped a small book into Joe Bob's hand. It was something he thought Joe Bob and his lovely wife-to-be should examine in private, since it had the answers to many of the questions that young people have, but are reluctant to ask.

"Thank you," Joe Bob said. "Thank you very much for your trouble." He walked out of the pastor's office with a smug expression on his face, as if he had received a personal compliment. Gladys was flustered and annoyed.

"Who does he think he is, talking to us that way?" She felt they'd been singled out. "Does he talk to everybody that way?"

"Of course he does," said Joe Bob. "That's his job." He tried to get her to look at the little book even before they were married, sitting on the porch that evening. She pretended to take it all seriously. "That's very interesting," she said over and over. Joe Bob showed her a drawing of an erect male member. There wasn't much detail. The style of drawing was the same as in the Time-Life how-to books where a person can learn how to make the basement into a rec room or insulate the attic.

"Well, that's all very interesting," she said.

Now that she had left Joe Bob and come home, when the pastor asked how she was, she told him, "Fine. I'm fine."

"I hope we see that husband of yours in church someday soon."

"Oh, yes. I expect maybe soon," said Gladys, arm in

arm with her large parents. They beamed and smiled down at her little blond head.

"Yes," her father said. "We have to get after that boy." They didn't say a word about the separation. Why should they? They were private people, and didn't feel obliged to share their worries and problems with the whole congregation at First Baptist.

They were more comfortable, in fact, with the religious services that they saw on television than those at their neighborhood church. Jerry Falwell and Pat Robertson seemed wiser than Pastor Eckland. More on top of things. On the television they saw the harmony that they tried to create in their own little home. Everything clean and bright and in its place. When the camera panned over the audience, Gladys would sit up and watch attentively, studying the handsome, two-parent families with their children. The women she liked particularly, lifting their hands with sweet gentle smiles as they prayed. Sometimes she and her parents talked about responding to one of the appeals for support. Mrs. Posner, particularly, was always touched by those clips of missionaries with starving black babies.

"Couldn't we give something?" she would say to her husband.

He would shake his head with a sad smile.

"Charity begins at home," he would say, and look around the small room with its clean paint, its white plaster moldings. Well of course it did. How much could they do to help the suffering of the world? Not very much, when you stopped to think about it. At moments like this, it seemed to Gladys, it was their duty simply to *be*. To go on as they were, happy and at peace.

One evening, however, they saw something that disturbed Gladys very much. A church in Florida was having a revival service conducted by an evangelist from England. He was a young man with a heavy, sensuous face, but enormous dignity. He spoke in an even, magisterial voice, with a beautiful accent, as he paced before the congregation. When sweat would accumulate on his forehead or upper lip, he would blot it with a clean white handkerchief, still folded into a neat square. Gladys held her breath. He looked just like Joe Bob. She snuck a glance at her mother and father to see if they'd noticed. She was sure she'd be able to tell. But their bland, handsome faces gave nothing away. They seemed enchanted. She opened her mouth to make some comment, but couldn't think of anything to say. She hadn't really been listening to what the minister was talking about. Perhaps no one was. Perhaps it wasn't important.

At that moment, someone in the television audience began to laugh. Gladys felt her face go rigid in the way it did when there was something unpleasant to be ignored. She could feel her mouth assume a polite, attentive smile. Out of the corner of her eye she saw that her parents were smiling in the same way. They were focusing on the preacher and leaving it to the ushers in the church to take care of the disturbance. There must have been a real security problem in that church, Gladys decided, because the laughing got worse. The camera panned over the audience, and focused on a man in a starched white shirt. He was trying to contain himself, but obviously something hilarious was going on somewhere. Tears of amusement were simply streaming down his face. Where were those security people? Couldn't they do their jobs? Or was it simply too much for them? The camera crew were certainly no help. They seemed to be deliberately seeking out the little pockets of hilarity and broadcasting them to the entire viewing world. What *were* they laughing at, Gladys wondered. Was it the evangelist's accent? Gladys had a terrible thought: What was he going to think of American audiences? They were probably going to show this program on the evening news all over Europe. Gladys kept the little smile fixed to her face, but the thought of the international implications was making it tremble.

When another minister came on the screen with an appeal for donations, Mrs. Posner excused herself and went into the kitchen. Mr. Posner got out the little tables on which they had supper in front of the television. These were kept folded in the closet during the day, but when it was time to eat, her father would set them up in a semi-circle. They were made of tubular metal with a tray that snapped down on top. The trays had floral arrangements stenciled on them. The one Gladys preferred was decorated with a pattern of hollyhocks. It was her tray so to speak, but that evening her father took it for himself.

"Well, I'm glad that's over," said Gladys, stiff with irritation.

"What?"

"That program. Didn't you think that laughing and carrying on about that man's accent was a little uncalled for?" She squirmed in her chair, feeling she had broken some rule even bringing the matter up. No, it was much better just to let the occasional unpleasantness that one encountered drift by. You didn't make things better by dwelling on the dark side of things.

"Oh, they weren't laughing at the minister," her father said.

"It sounded like it to me."

"Oh, no, no, no," said Mr. Posner, running his broad hands over the hollyhocks on the tray with evident pleasure. He explained that the congregation was laughing because they were so overjoyed. They couldn't contain themselves because they felt so good. Gladys didn't know whether to believe him or not, but when her mother came in, she confirmed what her father had said.

"They're *supposed* to laugh. The minister would have been really disappointed if they didn't."

"Gladys thought they were laughing at his accent," said her father.

"No, dear," said her mother, putting down a plate of roast pork and applesauce on her tray table. "Didn't you see this program in Clarence?" she asked, a little edge to her voice. "When you were watching Christian television? It's been on regularly for some time. It was all explained."

"No," said Gladys. "I never saw anything like this." She felt a flush climb her throat as her parents digested this information. "I think Clarence has a different cable system."

"That would explain why you never saw it," said her father, taking a big bite of meat.

Gladys turned her face toward the picture window. It was growing dark. Beyond the garden was the dark wood with its secret herd of hungry deer. Already they might be gathering at the wood's edge, ready to creep out. All of her serenity, her fragile happiness, seemed to dissolve away. "What am I going to do," Gladys whispered. "What will happen to me?"

On her nineteenth birthday, a mysterious package arrived in the mail. Gladys found her mother by the front door, studying a brown paper parcel that she held firmly by the ends.

"Who's that from?" Gladys asked.

"Well, I don't know," said her mother, almost laughing with aggravation. When Gladys saw the label she understood her mother's confusion. It was one of those multi-layered packing labels where the addresses and names grow fainter and fainter as the various layers of duplicating paper are stripped away. Mrs. Posner assumed that the last layer but one—the one she had signed—must have contained a legible return address, but she had been so flustered at the moment of affixing her name to the package that she hadn't noticed. It had never been clear to her, exactly, to what she was committing herself when she took the delivery person's ballpoint pen in her own hand and wrote firmly by the x, Mrs. Irwin Posner. Consequently, she was somewhat nervous and distracted. "It must be for you, Gladys. For your birthday," she declared. "It must be from your Uncle Herbert."

It would be unusual for Herbert Posner to send his niece a package. Ordinarily he sent a card picked out at the local supermarket together with a small check, often with some small message on the memo line next to his signature. "Don't spend it all in one place!" he might write, or "Buy American!" But if it wasn't from Uncle Herbert, then it wasn't clear who it might be from. Birthdays at the Posners were observed with some care and intensity, but very privately. When Gladys had been very young, she was allowed to invite two or three friends over for cake and ice cream, and photographs were taken and exclaimed over. "Do you remember that year you spilled ice cream in your lap?" her father might say. "Those were the days."

Still, it had been a relief when Gladys had decided she wanted just her parents at her party. "Just us three are enough," she said firmly when her mother protested faintly. When she'd turned sixteen there hadn't been a person in the high school who knew. For some reason she never clearly understood, she relished this secret, as if it represented a significant triumph over the demands of the outside world.

"What if it's from Joe Bob?" Gladys said, unable to contain herself. What if it's a bomb? she wanted to ask. She felt she deserved it, running off the way she had.

"Joe Bob?" said her mother, frowning. "Oh, I don't think so." She put the parcel down carefully on the washstand underneath the mirror where a person could check her appearance before she went outside. "I don't think he would send anything," she said, without explaining her grounds.

"I think I'll open it," said Gladys, her fingers scrabbling over the slippery paper. "There's probably a card inside." She expected to find some attractive wrapping paper underneath the tough brown outer layer. Perhaps even a crushed bow done up with shiny ribbons. But inside was a simple red box with "Caruso's Marzipan Garden" printed on the outside. Since there was no gift wrap, there seemed to be no reason not to simply go ahead and open the box and see if there really was marzipan inside. Gladys pried up the lid and revealed a tray of imitation vegetables. Carrots and little turnips, potatoes and tomatoes, all molded out of almond paste, and nestled in shredded green cellophane. The potatoes were the most lifelike, if that was the right word, with imitation potato eyes, and a skin dusted with cinnamon. There was also a large purple eggplant. Gladys felt a spasm in her bowels. The room swam. She wanted to sit down.

"I don't think this is for you at all," said her mother. "It must be for your father. Probably one of his clients." Mr. Posner was a CPA and often received gifts from people, grateful because he had saved them some unexpected amount on their income tax in a perfectly legitimate way. His wife began to fuss, worried because now there would be a person they saw regularly at church or the store who would expect some expression of gratitude, but who was probably too polite to say anything if none was forthcoming.

"You must be right," said Gladys, pulling herself together. She rewrapped the package as best she could. "I don't think anyone would send me marzipan. I don't even like it."

In her heart, she was sure the box was from Joe Bob. It would be just the sort of thing he would send. Something picked out to convey a hidden message that she wouldn't really understand. He'd forget to have it gift wrapped, of course, and was incapable of doing it himself. She could picture him laboring over some elaborate gift wrap, and then simply giving up and swathing the package with brown paper and Scotch tape. He was remarkably un-handy in some respects, not even knowing the trick for curling the ends of a ribbon with one of the blades of a pair of scissors.

That night for supper they had all her favorite things. All the food she'd ever asked for as a special treat. Scallops with a strip of bacon pinned around them with a tooth-pick, cloverleaf rolls, twenty-four hour salad, stuffed pork chops, stuffed mushrooms, stuffed peppers, sticky buns (without the cinnamon, of course). It was as if every birthday meal she'd ever had had to be eaten all over again.

Her parents' present was a promise to redecorate her bedroom. Her mother took her hand and promised new window treatments and carpets. She could even have a brand-new bed if she wanted.

Gladys protested that she loved her bed just as it was. She'd had it since she was ten years old.

"You're a grown woman now. Not a little girl. It's time you worked out a new self-image," said her father and passed around the box of marzipan vegetables. He picked out a carrot for himself and bit into it with his regular, somewhat glassy dentures.

"I think I like the potatoes the best," he said, chewing.

"I think they must all taste exactly the same," said Gladys. To hear his finger rooting in the cellophane grass made her want to scream. She felt stuffed with what she'd eaten, filled with food right to the back of her throat.

"No. The potatoes are more minty. I think the carrots have a licorice taste," said Mr. Posner.

"They all taste exactly the same," insisted Gladys wildly and fled the room.

"This is getting to be a pattern," she heard her father say when she was somewhere in the dark space between the door to the living room and the foot of the stair.

Thinking back, she realized it must have been about this time that the stealing started. That's how she thought of it. Not that she stole something. Rather it was something that happened to her, or possibly merely in her presence. Sometimes she half pretended to herself that she was psychically gifted. Like those young girls (usually virgins!) who are sometimes the focus of poltergeist activity. Around me, she thought, things get stolen.

She stole small things. Lipstick, bottles of nail polish, Chap Sticks, batteries, key chains, magazines and pocketbooks, pairs of gloves or packages of stockings. Ordinarily she would slip an item quite openly into her pocket or bag. Often, she would simply carry it away in her hand. That seemed bold. She thought, too, she might always claim absentmindedness if confronted, and indeed there was something trancelike about her behavior when the mood was on her. She would enter a store, preferably one at the mall where she could wander from place to place with her coat over her arm. She would pick things up and put them down, ponder innocent cosmetics, rolls of cellophane tape, racks of markers and ballpoint pens. When she sauntered out she might have any number of things in her bag, under the folds of her coat, in her hand.

"I was looking for the cash register," she thought she might say if she was asked. She felt quite calm, even innocent.

Only later, contemplating her loot in the car or—this was better—at home on her bed, would the enormity of the risks she was taking strike her. Her face would burn and her hands tremble. She could hardly breathe. This was how a thief gives herself away, she thought. The trembling, the furtive look-round, the red face, the hurried step. They've already been tried and convicted in their own minds. It's like a lie detector test. A person who doesn't want to lie is the one who gets caught. A good liar, one who is comfortable with his fictions, is quite safe.

She enjoyed showing the things she had taken to her mother and father. This was the best part in a way. "Do you think this is a nice shade of lipstick?" she might ask. "I thought it might go with my coloring." She liked to see the stolen tube in her mother's hands. The cap pulled off, the wedge of greasy color rising as its base was twisted. "Very nice," her mother might say.

It was because Mrs. Posner had a certain loyalty to a carpet company that hadn't had enough sense to move out to the suburbs that Gladys was finally caught. Branded a shoplifter by that awful woman with the red glasses. She would never have gone into that part of town on her own. The Arkadian Carpet Company and the neighboring row of antique shops looked respectable enough, but right around the corner was a Community Food Kitchen with homeless men and women waiting outside to be fed. When Gladys drove by, they were talking and smoking cigarettes, not the least ashamed. She drove blocks to find a place to park.

When she made a comment to Mr. Arkadian about the lack of secure parking facilities, he wasn't at all sympathetic. He had stayed in the same storefront for fifty years.

"It's all in your head," he told her. "There's nothing here to be afraid of."

While Gladys looked over the carpet samples in the littered front room, he went into the back of the shop and began to cook some elaborate foreign dish on a hot plate. That seemed very rude to her. A garlicky, spicy smell came wafting through the old maroon curtains that hung over the doorway and clung, she was sure, to her clothes. Her fingers were raw from turning over the heavy pieces of carpet. When she looked at them, she saw they'd become shiny and gray, as if polished with dirt.

"Oh, Mr. Arkadian?" she said, going to the doorway and pulling aside one of the curtains. He was stirring onions in a skillet, a dish towel tucked in his belt. "Is that all the sculpted carpet you have in those samples? I really wanted something more of a peach color." She wanted to embarrass him a little. She thought he should be out helping her turn over the heavy books of carpet instead of frying onions.

"That was a nice peach color I showed your mother when I came out to the house," he said, deftly tipping the onions into an aluminum pot.

"Yes, but that wasn't sculpted. I wanted it sculpted."

"You won't find that color in sculpted carpet. What I've got is right out there." He pointed with his spoon past her shoulder to the unwieldy pile through which she had been searching. Her shoulders ached to look at it. Her mouth felt as if it had been filled with dust. Through the clouded windows of the front of the shop she could see poor people walking by.

"I think I'll come back another time," Gladys said as sharply as she could. She wanted him to understand that he had just lost a customer. That she could find exactly what she wanted in one of those bright, clean stores out on Sheridan Road.

On the street, the bright sun confused her for a moment, and she wasn't sure where she'd left the car. She started walking north, toward the Symphony Circle area, but almost at once realized she was going in the wrong direction. It was when she'd turned around that she'd seen the drunk man coming at her. He was pulling at the crotch of his pants, and suddenly she got a whiff of him. The smell was terrible. She felt physically defiled, and wasn't it true in a way? That she could smell him at all meant that some of his molecules had gotten up her nose.

Microscopic pieces of his body. Was it any surprise she simply ran into the first convenient shop? She was in distress. She never would have gone in there otherwise. And then, standing in that dark cluttered place, full of all sorts of old things...anybody would have gotten confused. She'd picked up that perfume bottle merely to show an interest and be polite. She couldn't help it if she forgot to put it down. That's what forgetting means! She couldn't help it! What if she'd picked up some of the litter from the floor? She supposed they would have accused her of trying to steal that, too. In fact, however, there was absolutely nothing in that whole establishment that she would give house room to. Taking some of it hardly seemed a crime. It seemed a kind of fraud to try to sell it.

Well, it was all over now.

Gladys sat up on her bed and wiped her eyes. She blew her nose. She had a cold coming on. She probably caught it when she smelled that drunk man. But it was really and truly all over now with no harm done. That was what she had to tell herself. She wouldn't even have to see that man and the woman with the funny glasses again. A curious peace descended jerkily around her, like a stage curtain let down awkwardly between the past and the future.

She had certainly learned her lesson! she thought. No more taking things. Not even by accident. It was that simple. Oh, she knew it could have been much worse. What if that man had really called the police? She'd have a record, then. No escaping that. It would all be *real*. Now, sitting on her dear familiar bed, all those things she'd stolen seemed to fade like old memories and lose their substance. She'd been lucky. No doubt about it. Saved from a life of crime. She felt blessed.

At supper that evening, both Mr. and Mrs. Posner noticed the difference in her attitude. She seemed genuinely happy. Full of light and little jokes. Just like the old days. She told them the story about Mr. Arkadian cooking his supper on a hot plate. She made it sound like an adventure, as if she'd gone off and visited a foreign country right in their own city. Mr. Posner patted his daughter's hand.

"I'm sure you can get sculpted carpet in any shade you want right out here in North Tonawanda," he said.

A shade, like some hidden misgiving, passed over his wife's face. Gladys saw it, and felt a stab of panic.

"Don't you think I can, Mama?" asked Gladys. "Do I have to go back to that store?"

"Oh, no, darling," said her mother. "I was thinking of something else."

"Of what? What were you thinking of, Mama?"

"Well, of all that garlic. That's what I was thinking of. How its smell gets into things," said Mrs. Posner, and blushed. Her husband and daughter couldn't help laughing at the face she made. They leaned back in their chairs and smiled and nodded at one another. The little house was warm and smelled of baking. The polished linoleum floors gleamed. Everything was in its place at last.

"Oh look," said Gladys suddenly, turning her bright face to the picture window. "It's getting dark out."

She got up and drew the curtain so no one could see.

Smoke

JOAN BAUER

TO: ALL MCK EMPLOYEES
FROM: Rupert Sack
SUBJECT: NEW CLIENT

Please join us in welcoming Fortune 100's Engell Corporation to our growing list of blue-chip clients. Engell
has distinguished itself as an innovative leader in con-
sumer package goods and community outreach. We
are excited to be part of the advertising team that will
spearhead Engell's vision of excellence and leader-
ship into the global arena.

I'm reading this e-mail and trying to hang my winged
pig poster on the wall of my cubicle at the same time. I
hold the pig in place, which isn't easy—the hook keeps
slipping. I try to reach the mouse with my foot.
Click.

Crane my neck to read.

TO: ALL SUMMER INTERNS
FROM: Cara Robbins, Assistant Personnel Director
SUBJECT: YOUR FIRST DAY!

We at MCK welcome you and hope that your summer
with us will be exciting, personally meaningful, and
instructive! We will do everything to tap your gifts and
help you grow in this exciting creative environment.
As our CEO Rupert Sack has said, if we're not committed to the next generation, we have no business
doing business! Attached you will find the schedule
for your exciting first day!! ☺

I hate smiley faces. They deny the pain of humanity.
Reduce us all to bald, grinning morons.

The pig is hung.

I hit REPLY. Type, Thank you. This is so exciting . . . Annie ☺

That's when Julian comes in.

"You know, Annie, that's really my pig, too."

"Spare me, Julian."

Julian is my ex-boyfriend with whom I parted amica-
bly, even though he remains brick thick as to *why* we
broke up. We both landed intern jobs here.

"I found that pig, Annie. I paid for part of it."

"I gave you the money, Julian. You never paid me
back."

"But I plan to someday."

"And when might that be?"

He looks at the flying pig.

We both know the truth.

I study myself in the little mirror my uncle Farley gave me. During the last year of his life, when Uncle Farley looked as bad as a human being can, he always told me, "If you can't look good, at least look sincere."

My skin is pale, my hair is lifeless, but I haven't lost sincere.

"You've got more mail." Julian clicks *my* mouse.

TO: ANNIE BOSWELL
FROM: Rick Logan, Director of Security
SUBJECT: NONDISCLOSURE STATEMENT

Dear New Employee,

This is to inform you that all company and client mate-rial is confidential and is not to be communicated in any form—printed, electronic, or verbal—to anyone outside the firm without specific authorization of your supervisor. All creative work you do here is fully owned by MCK Advertising. Your complete five-page nondisclosure, work for hire, and electronic security statement is attached. Please print and sign before beginning any company assignments. Welcome aboard!

I press PRINT. The machine whirs.

Julian checks his watch. "I have to go." He checks my schedule. "And you have to go." Julian has deep control issues.

"I have to read this."

"I'll save you the trouble. It says if you doodle anything

meaningful on a napkin, they own it. If you talk in your sleep, they'll know. If you tell anyone about the brilliant advertising campaigns being planned here, they will make your life hell on earth."

• • •

Blue Room, MCK Advertising.

Present: Shana Krill, creative director; Melanie Tobias and Kevin Lynch, copywriters; and me, lowly summer intern of zero influence.

Shana: "We need to revamp the TV campaign for Bright and Beautiful shampoo; freshen up the image. We've had the same redhead washing her hair for ages. Thoughts...? And Annie, do feel free to jump in."

Melanie: "Bring in a blonde."

I shift in my chair. As a brunette, I resent that.

Kevin: "Blonde, young, energetic."

I groan internally. That's like every other shampoo ad.

Shana: "Is there something that would turn this around? Give us a new face?"

I raise my hand nervously. I'm not always this brave.

"Annie..."

"Change the name...?"

Shana: "Bright and Beautiful is *known*, Annie. We'd be starting from zero."

Me: "But, it sounds kind of old-fashioned. If you change the name to Shine On and say it's *from* Bright and Beautiful; if you had a great-looking woman who's a dirt-bike racer, and she's racing this guy, and it's clear he's trying to push her off the road, but she's jumping over puddles and getting filthy and some of the dirt is in her hair... but it still looks decent. Then she passes him and then we see her washing it, and it looks *fabulous*. It makes the shampoo seem more . . . fun."

They look at me. I'm not sure where all that came from.

Shana: "I love that. Has there ever been a shampoo spot where a model gets her hair dirty?"

Melanie: "I don't think so."

Kevin: "I don't think she has to *pass* the guy."

Melanie: "He could just fall off his bike and lie helpless in a ditch."

Me, pumped: "You could have a series of ads where women get their hair dirty in funny ways."

Melanie: "They could be painting a ceiling and get paint splattered in their face."

Kevin: "There could be a young mom holding a baby. The baby's got sticky hands and is grabbing the mother's hair."

It went on like this for two hours.

Like playing racquetball with ideas.

I have *always* wanted to be in advertising.

Shana takes me aside. "I'd like you to sit in on a lunch meeting today, Annie."

Wow. "I'd love to."

"And don't hold back. I want to hear your thoughts."

I nod creatively.

Head back to my cube.

Face the pig.

Yes!

• • •

Green Room, MCK Advertising.

Fresh mozzarella and focaccia sandwiches. Strawberries. White-chocolate chip cookies, excellent ice tea. This is heaven, I swear.

Riley Paris, account manager: "You like the tea?"

We murmur yes.

"We need to name the tea. It's our new account."

I feel the flow of creative heat permeate the room.

Everyone drinks more tea.

Shana: "It's a strong flavor."

Riley Paris: "This one's ginger. They don't mess around."

Shana: "Forceful. Satisfying. Not for wimps. None of these are right."

Another woman: "Today's Ice Tea. Tomorrow's Ice Tea. Yesterday's Ice Tea for Today."

That's bad.

Shana: "What's the company's name?"

Riley Paris: "Benninger Beverages."

I raise my hand.

Shana leans forward.

"Excellent Ice Tea," I say.

Riley Paris: "I *like* that."

Me: "Wait. Even better. *Uncle Benny's* Excellent Ice Tea."

That other woman: "Sounds too much like Uncle Ben's rice."

Riley Paris: "I like it."

Shana: "We could cast for Uncle Benny. Make him like Colonel Sanders."

Me: "Or he could just be cool-looking. A cool guy
who makes great ice tea."

They look at me.

I smile sincerely.

I stink at sports.

I've never once balanced my checkbook.

I can't seem to keep a boyfriend for over three months.

But I've always been quick at thinking things up.

I feel like a wanderer who has found the way home.

• • •

"Annie..." Julian grabs my arm. "I looked for you at
lunch. Where were you?"

I tell him.

"They *fed* you?" Free food is important to Julian.

"And I have a three o'clock meeting on another product."

"Will they feed you again?"

"I don't know, Julian."

"If you make vice president, don't forget the little people who helped you on the path, thinking nothing of
themselves."

• • •

Green Room again.

No food.

Me, Shana, Melanie, Kevin.

Shana: "We have a new product that we want to show-
case. We want deep entrenchment of the name. On the
lips of those who need it. Something that says, 'Young
and Exciting. Audacious and Courageous. A little risky,
but not illegal, not dangerous. Definitely not dangerous.'"

Melanie laughs. Kevin looks clueless.

I raise my hand. "What's the product?"

Shana: "Right now, we're not talking product, Annie. We're just tossing concepts around."

I don't know what she's talking about, but I nod like I toss concepts in my sleep.

Melanie: "I'll just throw out *Extreme. No boundaries.*"

Shana: "Let's get personal. A statement about life."

Kevin: "Okay, we're all *challenged, focused, determined.*"

Shana: "Give me more 'Road Less Traveled' kind of thoughts, but adapted for today."

Kevin: "To go where no man has gone before."

Shana: "That's been done."

Melanie: "To take a new, divergent path. To just *go for it.* To just *be there.* To just, I don't know, *be...*"

I raise my hand. "Bold," I offer. "Be bold."

They look at me.

I add, "People want to think of themselves as bold."

Shana writes BOLD—BE BOLD with a purple marker on the white board. "It's crossethnic, crossgenerational. Let's put something more together. How could we carry 'Be bold' into, say, print?"

Me: "You could have a group of intense people who look like a Gap ad standing by a mountain. I think having a community of people together, like friends, is an important message. We're bold with our friends—we share this together. And the whole group is holding up their hands like they've just won something. *Be bold.*"

Shana is taking notes furiously.

Melanie: "Or you could have people climbing a mountain together."

Kevin: "We could have people deep-sea diving. . . ."

Shana: "You can't use the product underwater."

Kevin: "Can you use it in a boat?"

Shana: "Yes."

Kevin: "Sailing then. A bunch of friends on a yacht . . ."

Shana: "Flat stomachs, white teeth. Healthy glow."

Kevin: "We see the boat from the back. The *Be Bold*."

Shana: "What if the product has a blue stripe on it?"

Melanie: "Like a racing stripe . . ."

Me: "Bold Blue."

Shana grins. "That's it! And since the product comes in multiples, we call it, Bold Blues."

I have to admit, that has a ring to it.

"Brilliant work, everyone." Shana nods at me, grabs her notes, and hurries out the door.

I sit there while the others leave.

You can do so much with a few words.

I used to write my own greeting cards. I'd have one word on the card—Hope. Inside I'd write, *Keep hoping.* Or I'd think of something grim—PMS. Inside I'd write, *No male will ever understand this. I'm glad we're friends.* The right words bind us together. So many of my friends kept the Hope and PMS cards. My best friend, Reena, said I should combine them since hope is something you really need during PMS.

I write *Be Bold* on my notepad and walk boldly back to my cube.

• • •

End of the day. 5:40.

I am energized, focused.

Julian is balancing a pretzel on his not inconsiderable nose.

He jerks his head, the pretzel pops in the air, he catches it in his mouth, almost knocks over my mirror from Uncle Farley. He steadies it—knows the history. He came to the funeral with me.

"Sorry, Annie."

A contingent of caterers walks by holding trays of little sandwiches and cakes. There's a meeting for some of the top execs from Engell Corporation in the MCK board-room. It seems like a big part of advertising is eating well.

A man with a huge vase of fresh cut flowers follows the caterers.

Julian watches the parade longingly.

"Julian, what does the Engell Corporation do?"

"I'm not sure. I've heard the name a lot." He's foraging in my desk drawers. "Where's your emergency chocolate?"

"In the bottom at the back."

I sit at the computer, type in www.engellcorporation.com.

On the screen, the Web site.

A stock-market ticker proclaims the stock is hot and rising.

A Press Page proclaims its executives are caring and innovative.

"Engell," the CEO writes, "is a responsible corporate community. We are proud to sponsor a multimillion-dollar campaign to discourage underage smoking. Smoking is a very personal decision and should be made only by adults. And while we are against any marketing manipulation of children, we envision a more tolerant world where smokers have rights, too."

"Julian..." He's on his knees, rifling the bottom drawer. *"Forget the chocolate."*

"Never."

"Julian—look at this!"

He does. I flop back in my chair. My mouth feels dry. He clicks the mouse by *Our Products.*

On the screen now, the hugely popular cigarettes manufactured by the Engell Corporation:

Slimmers
Candy Man
Caribbean Breeze Menthols
Quentin and Rhodes—Regular and Low Tar

Julian puts his hand on my shoulder.

My uncle Farley died from emphysema.

Left a wife and two kids.

At the end of his life, he was close to blue and could hardly breathe.

Then the thought hits me.

Bold Blues.

I thought that up today.

I tell Julian about the meeting. Start to cry.

"My God, Julian, I think I might have named a cigarette!"

"You don't know that for sure."

He scrolls down to a box, *Stamp It Out, Kids.*

Audio: "Now, when Engell Corporation says we're serious about young people not smoking, we're not just blowing smoke."

The screen explodes into black-and-purple graphics. Young dancers twirl and stomp to the sounds of drumbeats.

The dancers freeze and shout, *"Stamp it out!"* They gesture as if they're putting out a cigarette, shout, *"Stamp it out!"* At this point, Melanie Rears—a hot young pop singer—dances onscreen, shouting *"Stamp it out, kids! Stamp it out!"* Behind her is the calendar of her spring tour, sponsored by Quentin and Rhodes Tobacco.

Then, on the screen come the friendly questions:

WHAT ARE YOU ABOUT?
Where do you and your friends like to hang out most?
Where wouldn't you be caught dead in public even if
     you were in disguise?
The best place to buy clothes—so, where is it?
The best place to eat—come on, tell us.

They're doing market research to find out what kids like and where they go.

Julian prints out the page.

"Let's do more of this, Annie, but just not here."

. . .

My house. My computer.

Try to sit. Can't. Try to stand. Can't.

I can pace.

Julian is doing an online search, finding terrifying factoids about Big Tobacco.

"Okay, we're entering into deep space with these sleazeballs. Projectile vomiting is appropriate. We begin with a quote from the Shame on Them Hall of Fame. 'What, if anything, can be done to turn around or slow down the erosion in the public acceptability of smoking?' That's from Hamish Maxwell, chairman and CEO of Philip Morris Companies Inc., to H. Burson, chairman and CEO of the PR firm Burson-Marsteller."

Julian's looking through Web sites. "Here's a history of how Big Tobacco plays the game. They'd take an absolute truth—secondhand smoke is dangerous. The EPA classifies secondhand smoke as a Class A carcinogen (causes cancer), which is good enough for most people with SATs of 300 and over. And they'd spin it around...say EPA's testing was flawed. They'd discredit the scientists who did the research. Now after all the lawsuits coming at them, they say oops, the EPA was right—cigarettes are dangerous, but we're responsible corporate citizens, blah, blah, blah." Julian clicks, shakes his head. "Here's another one. They say they obey the 1998 tobacco settlement that forbids marketing to kids. But, according to the *New England Journal of Medicine*, tobacco advertising in magazines popular with kids increased after the settlement."

I stand behind him. Look at the screen.

For more disgusting quotes, appalling facts and figures, click here.

I do.

Up pop links to the *Campaign for Tobacco-Free Kids,* the *American Nonsmokers' Rights Foundation.*

For Julian's personal message, click here.

I click.

Julian is so great.

Why did I break up with him?

As you can see, Annie, I continue to be sensitive and thoughtful, even in the midst of nefarious bad guys and evildoings.

Why did you break up with me?

It was the pig, wasn't it?

I laugh through tears. You know how that goes.

· · ·

I've had a grand total of two hours' sleep. We talked till 1 A.M. My mom joined us. She's scrambling eggs this morning to make me strong.

I'm going to work today. I'm going to confront them.

I need this job badly, too, to save money for college.

Mom says, "Do you want me to go with you?"

"I want a Doberman to go with me."

"Don't discredit the fierceness of mothers."

"I need to do this myself, Mom."

"Call me."

"I will."

· · ·

"For what it's worth, Annie, you're doing the right thing."

Julian kisses my hand like I'm a princess.

I walk into the Green Room for the morning creative meeting.

"Okay, everyone, we are hot, I'm telling you." Shana stands in front of the white board that has BE BOLD and BOLD BLUES written in block letters. "The account team went *crazy* for this. We want to take it further, *bolder*." She grins at me.

"We want to achieve the ultimate here—create an ad campaign *without* running any ads."

Kevin: "Is the budget big?"

Shana: "Huge."

Kevin: "What's the target audience?"

Shana: "Teen to twenty-five."

Melanie: "We pay some hot actor to walk around with the product. Send the photos to *People,* that kind of thing."

Shana: "We're thinking about going grassroots. Young actors—*very* with it—seen with the product outside movie theaters, outside big rock concerts. A role model approach in city to city. How do we get *Be Bold* across?"

I stand up. "Are we talking about cigarettes?"

Shana: "I'm really not at liberty to say, Annie. We're just batting ideas around."

I sit back down, feel like a coward.

Hate myself for doing that.

Kevin: "We could have people scrawl *Be Bold* like graffiti on walls and sidewalks all over the country."

I sit there.

Think of Uncle Farley's funeral. All the relatives gathered.

Four people in my family quit smoking that day. My mom couldn't stop crying—Farley was her big brother. The best guy, too. Forty-six years old. He'd been smoking since he was fifteen.

Melanie: "I think entrenchment of the product comes like D-Day. Hit everywhere at once. On the beach, at the mall, at the movies, at record stores, at concerts, photo ops in the right magazines."

I sit here even though I want to run.

Working the words I need to say over and over in my mind.

Shana stands up, heads for the door. Melanie and Kevin leave.

I stand. "Shana, I have to talk to you."

"I've got to run this by—"

"Shana, I have a right to know the product I'm being asked to work on."

She closes the door. "There's a lot that happens in advertising that's confidential."

"Please tell me."

"Annie, you've done some fine work for us. You have a quick mind and a real gift for getting to the punch of a message."

"What's the product, Shana?" I hand her the pages from Engell Corporation's Web site.

She sighs deep. "It's . . . a new cigarette . . . very low tar . . . the low tar is going to actually help people, Annie."

"My uncle died from emphysema, Shana. He smoked low tar cigarettes for years. Low tar is a joke."

"That's a bit harsh, Annie."

"His funeral was *harsh*. The fact that he couldn't quit because cigarettes are addictive is *harsh*. The fact that his kids are growing up without a dad is—"

Shana throws up her hands. "I just work on the copy—direct the creative flow. I'm not a scientist. I'm not a doctor. I'm not making any claims here. I haven't created the product; I just look for the best way to tell people it's out there. If we weren't working on this, believe me, a hundred other ad agencies would pounce on this business."

• • •

I stand in Cara Robbins's office.

"I was not told I was working on a cigarette campaign. If I'd known, I would have refused to be part of it. I want my ideas back."

"Annie, we've never had this happen with an intern before. Interns just usually, well—"

"Get abused. I try to be a trendsetter. Monica Lewinsky is not my patron saint."

Her phone rings. She answers, listens, stunned by the news.

"Annie, *Rupert Sack* wants to talk to you right now."

When I do not show proper awe and reverence, she says, "Mr. Sack is *very* busy and *important*."

• • •

Julian is not in his cube.

I'm trying to organize my thoughts. But the only thoughts I have are perfectly clear.

Smoking kills people.

Creating hidden marketing campaigns so more people will smoke is immoral.

I was manipulated into being part of that.

I head down the hall to Rupert Sack's office.

Feel like Dorothy going to see the Wizard of Oz.

Except I've got no Tin Man, no Lion, no Scarecrow, and no magic slippers.

• • •

"Annie, I've been hearing about you all day." Rupert Sack looks sincerely at me, big grin. "Sit down."

I gulp. Try not to look around his enormous office. I sit in a very soft leather chair.

"I can honestly say, Annie, that I'm glad this issue came up. When we took the Engell Corporation as a client, I knew we'd be having some of these discussions. This is helping me. Thank you."

"You're welcome." He's really got sincere down.

"Annie, this is about realities. The realities of business. The realities of how this country works." He pauses here. "I know your uncle died from emphysema. I think I understand some of your feelings. My father died from lung cancer. But I know my dad would be proud of the campaign we're putting together for Engell. He always told me, 'Follow your heart. Be tolerant of other people. Respect the fact that everyone has strengths and weaknesses. Nobody's perfect.' He was a great man because he accepted his weaknesses. He used to kid me and say, 'Well, Rupe, if I wasn't smoking, I might not be coughing so much, but God knows, I might be beating your mother.' Are you following me?"

"I think so."

He walks over to a mahogany bookcase with gold awards on the shelves. "Do you know how many awards we've won at this agency for advertising excellence?"

"Looks like a lot."

He nods proudly. Looks out his enormous window at the Manhattan skyline. "Did you know that Engell gave millions of dollars to help stamp out hunger?"

"I saw that on their Web page."

"They are a corporate giant, Annie. They employ thousands of people worldwide, provide healthcare for untold numbers of families. They have college scholarships. They fund research and development at universities. Their stock has consistently performed in these hard economic times and helped many realize their retirement dreams."

"I don't see it the way you do, Mr. Sack. I don't think this country should manufacture something that's been proven to kill and hurt so many people."

"I appreciate your idealism, Annie. Don't lose it, just redefine it. Don't be so black-and-white. The world is full of gray areas. All kinds of things can kill people. A car can kill you—we advertise those. An airplane. The wrong medicine can kill you. A bee sting if you're an allergic person. A chicken bone can kill you—we don't hold back advertising poultry. Frank Perdue rose from the coop to become a household word. My sister is allergic to peanuts.

If one sneaks in, she swells up like the Poppin' Fresh doughboy. It's a tough world out there. People make choices. Choices to drink, choices to drive too fast, choices to smoke or not to smoke. We're not here to condemn or to say to any business, you have no right to the best advertising representation in the world.

"And you, Annie, have given us the seed to grow a responsible campaign that we will not abuse. I have children of my own. I don't want them to smoke, but tobacco isn't going away. So I like to think that I can make the world a better place by helping to advertise it responsibly."

"I was in that meeting, Mr. Sack. It seemed like most of what was being planned was going to be a sneak attack."

"Those creative meetings can get pretty emotional."

I give him the research Julian did on the Web. "The Tobacco Law of 1998 said tobacco companies can't directly advertise to children. But that meeting was looking for a way to get around that law."

Rupert Sack turns from the window. "What you heard in that meeting is strictly confidential. I am holding your signed five-page nondisclosure agreement as legal witness to that fact. But I'm also holding a bonus check for you, Annie. Seven thousand dollars for coming up with those great thoughts that we will fine-tune."

He hands me the check.

I've never even seen a check for seven thousand dollars.

I hand it back. "I can't take this."

"Why not?"

"Because I could never look at my uncle Farley's kids again. He got pneumonia at the end. Couldn't breathe, kept spitting up blood. He gathered us all in his room and said, 'Don't smoke.'"

"I'm not asking you to smoke, Annie. I'm asking you to do the job we hired you to do."

I couldn't believe I was saying it. "Mr. Sack, I quit."

"Don't make hair-trigger decisions. Sleep on it. Take the money."

"I couldn't sleep if I took the money. I'm like the princess and the pea. I'd know it was there somewhere."

"The princess and the pea is a fairy tale, Annie. The money is real."

I get up and head out the door.

• • •

I walk outside into the fresh air holding the pig and my mirror. Julian walks up to me.

"You quit, didn't you?"

I nod.

"Me, too."

"You're kidding?"

He shrugs.

"So what do we do now?" I ask.

"Be proud of what we did?"

"We're broke."

"Right."

"We're unemployed."

"Right."

"Does a nondisclosure agreement hold if we never got a salary?"

Julian looks at me.

"I mean, did they really employ us, if they didn't pay us?"

"I don't know. A lawyer would know."

"I think we need to get a lawyer, Julian. And then figure out the next step."

"You think there's a next step?"

"I think there probably is for me. I don't think I could watch Bold Blues come out and not tell someone what I know."

We walk past a group of young boys who are smoking Marlboros, trying to be cool.

I shout, "Hey, if you keep smoking your lungs will disintegrate and you'll spit blood in the street."

I get called several four-letter words, accompanied by universal hand gestures.

Julian laughs. "That certainly makes it all worthwhile."

He takes my hand. We walk down Madison Avenue.

So much hype in the world.

And it's so hard to see because of the smoke.

One Size Fits All

NIKKI GRIMES

Ordinary sin
is always in:
half-truths,
dragging God's name
through muddy places,
he-said, she-said gossip
otherwise known as
murder by mouth,
and on it goes.

But what the hey.
So maybe you color
outside the lines a time or two.
You figure God's busy
with bigger sins,

the heavier half
of the Big Ten.

Trouble is,
in the eternal equation,
size doesn't matter.
The wages of sin
is death.

Portrait of a Liar

NIKKI GRIMES

ACT I

Call them what you will:
fish tales, white lies, fibs.
Euphemisms notwithstanding,
none of us can claim
a clean tongue.

Take Jacob,
he who stole his brother's birthright—
a sly trade, cheap at twice the price.
One birthright for one bowl of warm stew
on a cold night.

Why not blame Esau, you say.
He was the one who played the fool.
True. But Jacob was no less the liar for it.

Ahh! I get it.
You don't yet see the lie.
Come closer.

Here's Jacob, see,
greedy for a greater blessing.
He conspires with his mother.
(Never mind whose idea it was.)
He slips into his parents' tent,
goes before his half-blind father
tricked out like his hairy brother,
sheepskin his disguise.
"Esau? Is that you?"
"Yes, Father," says Jacob.

Oh, the lies!
Jacob thought them clever.
Hear him snicker?

But that was years before
he found truth's table
turned on him.
The experience, I'm told, was grim.

ACT II

Enter Laban, a wiley old coot
as comfortable with subterfuge as Jake.
With one daughter too many,
Laban eyes Jacob eyeing his Rebekah,

and fires a plan.
"Young man," says he,
"slave—I mean, work for me
for seven years
and you will win a wife."

Our hero is no dummy.
He spies the spikes
of this thorny proposition.
Even so, the fire raging below
his waist propels him to accept.

Fast-forward seven years.
A tear in his eye,
our nervous groom fidgets at the altar.
The wedding march begins to play.
Laban's oldest, Leah,
makes her way down the aisle,
a conspiratorial smile hidden by her veil.
The lusty Jacob preens
for his sweet rose,
the lady he chose.
"Rebekah, is that you?"
"Yes, Jacob," says Leah.

And who is the author of this poetic justice?
The train of His robe
fills the temple with glory.

Good Deed

EMMA DONOGHUE

Sam had always thought of himself as a pretty decent guy, and who was to say he wasn't? While he was doing his MBA at the University of Toronto he'd been a volunteer on the Samaritans' phone line. These days he couldn't spare the time, but he made regular tax-free contributions to schemes for eradicating river blindness in Sub-Saharan Africa and improving children's sports facilities in the Yukon. He always wore a condom (well, not always, just when he was having sex), and he never pushed past old ladies to get on a streetcar.

The day it happened, he was coming down with a head cold. Funny how such a petty thing could make such a difference. Not that it felt petty at the time; it was a January cold, one of those brutes that made you screw up your eyes all week and cough wetly for the rest of the month. So Sam—sensibly enough—had left the office before rush hour in order to get home and take care of himself. He had his Windsmoor coat buttoned up to the throat as he hurried toward the subway station. His friends seemed to live in down jackets all winter, but Sam refused to abandon his dress sense so he could look like a walking duvet. Today he did keep his cashmere scarf looped over his nose and mouth, to take the ice out of the air. With a hot whiskey and *The X-Files* and an early night, he thought he could probably head this cold off at the pass.

He walked right by the first time, like everyone else. It was a common sight, these last few winters, street persons in sleeping bags lying on the hot air vents. The first time you saw it you thought: *My god, there's a guy lying in the middle of the sidewalk, and everyone's walking round him like he's invisible, how bizarre. What a sign of the times.* But you got used to it—and, to be fair, it was probably much warmer for the homeless, lying on the air vents, than if they had to tuck themselves away against the wall of a bank or a travel agency.

This particular guy near the intersection of Bloor and Bay seemed pretty much like all his peers: a crumpled bundle with eyes half-closed and a not-entirely-unsatisfied expression. *Probably Native,* thought Sam, *but you should never assume.* It was only when Sam had got as far as the crossing, blowing his nose on his handkerchief with awkward leather-gloved hands, that his brain registered what his eyes must have seen. Just as sometimes by the time you asked someone to repeat themselves, you had realized what they'd said. Anyway, that's when Sam saw it in his mind's eye, the little trickle of blood. He thought he must have imagined it. *Classic white-middle-class guilt hallucinations*, he said to himself. Then he thought: *So the guy's bleeding a little from the lip, not necessarily a big deal; I sometimes chew my lips to shreds when I'm working on a big presentation.*

The lights changed but something wouldn't let Sam cross. Instead, he clenched his jaw and waded back against the tide of commuters. He picked a place to stand, near enough to the street person to get a good look at him, but not so near that anyone would notice. Besides, if he stood too close the guy might wake up and take offense and bite him or something. A significant percentage of them were mentally ill, Sam had read in the *Street Times*, and no wonder, considering. But there was no sign of this particular guy waking up any time soon. The blood from his mouth had trickled all the way round and under his chin, now, like some kind of Frankenstein party makeup. He had a dirty white beard.

Sam had no idea what to do, and frankly, all he felt was irritation. Where were human feelings when you wanted them? The timing was so inappropriate. Why couldn't this have happened on another winter afternoon, when Sam didn't have a cold, and so would have been able to respond like the person he truly was?

His eyes were dripping; he thought they might freeze shut. He unfolded his handkerchief and mopped at his face. An unworthy thought occurred to him: *Why did I*

*look round at all, when I should have kept my head down
and run for the subway?*

There was a foul reek of spirits coming off the guy,
when Sam bent nearer. It occurred to him to touch the
guy, but he didn't know where. Or why, now Sam came to
think of it. On a theoretical level, he knew that the rigors
of life on the street would drive just about anyone to alco-
holism, but he still couldn't help finding it gross.

"Excuse me?" he said, sniffing loudly so his nose
wouldn't drip onto the guy. "Sir?" How ludicrously gen-
teel. "Mister? Are you OK?"

No answer. Sam's breath puffed out like white smoke.
He made up a reply: *Sure I'm OK, mister, I love to spend
my Friday nights lying on the sidewalk, bleeding from the
mouth.*

Sam was crouched beside the guy, now. Commuters
kept streaming past; nothing interrupted the flow on
Bloor and Bay. They probably assumed Sam was some
kind of weirdo friend of the guy on the ground, despite
the Windsmoor coat—which was trailing in the gutter's
mound of dirty old snow, he noticed, snatching up the
hem. Now that he wasn't upright and moving at speed,
like the commuters, it was as if he'd left the world of the
respectable and squatted in the mud. They'd probably
think the coat was stolen. Damn them for a bunch of cold
salaried bastards. It wouldn't occur to one of them to take
the time to stop and—

And what, exactly? What was Sam going to do?

His nose started running so fast he almost lost his balance as he rooted for his handkerchief. His legs were starting to freeze into place. He ripped one leather glove off, reared up, and blew his nose. It made the sound of a lost elephant.

Quick, quick, think. What about first aid? Shit, he should have volunteered to go on that in-house course last year. Shreds of traditional advice swam giddily through Sam's mind. Hot, sweet tea was his mother's remedy for everything, but it would be tough to come by; the nearest stall said *Espresso Express*. Whiskey? Hardly the thing if the guy was full of meths already. Put his feet higher than his head? What the fuck was that about? Sam wondered.

The guy on the ground hadn't moved. The blood didn't seem to be flowing at speed, exactly. It hadn't dripped onto the pavement yet. In films, bleeding from the mouth always meant you were a goner; the trickle only took a few seconds to grow into a terrible red river.

Sam shifted from foot to foot to keep his circulation going, like a hesitant dancer at an '80s disco night. Maybe, it occurred to him with an enormous wave of relief, maybe the blood on this guy's face was an old mark he hadn't washed off. If you didn't have a mirror you probably wouldn't even know you had blood on your chin. Maybe a bit of bleeding was the natural result of drinking meths or whatever the cocktail of choice was these days. Well, not choice; Sam didn't mean choice, exactly.

But the thing was, how could he be sure? How was a personnel officer with no medical experience to tell if there was something seriously wrong going on here? He shouldn't call 911 on a whim. If they sent an ambulance, it might be kept from some other part of the city where it was really needed. They got these mistaken call-outs all the time; hadn't he seen something on Citytv about it? And the homeless guy probably wouldn't thank him for getting him dragged into the Emergency Room either. . . .

And then Sam looked at the guy on the ground, really looked for the first time; he felt a wave of nausea roll from the toes he could no longer feel, all the way to his tightening scalp. The man lay utterly still, not even shivering in the hard air that seemed liable to crystallize round them both any minute now. Sam was not repelled by the guy, exactly; what turned his stomach was the sudden thought that he himself, by some terrible knot of circumstances such as came down on successful people all the time (getting fired, divorce, drugs, breakdown), might someday end up lying on an air vent with people stepping round him and an overeducated ignorant prick in a Windsmoor coat standing round inventing excuses for not making the call that could save his life.

Sam reached for his cell phone, but the pocket of his coat was empty. At first he couldn't believe it; thought he'd been robbed. Then he remembered laying it down beside his computer after lunch. Today of all days! His head was made of mucus.

He dialed 911 from the phone box at the corner. He was afraid they wouldn't believe that it was an emergency—that they would hang up on him—so he sounded inappropriately angry, even when he was giving the address. "The guy looks seriously ill," he barked.

It hadn't occurred to Sam to wonder what he would do

once he had made the call. He hovered outside the phone
box, as if waiting for another turn. In a sense, there was
nothing else to do now; the proper authorities had been
called in, and Sam was just a passerby again, with every
right to head home to his condo and nurse his cold. But
in another sense, he thought with self-righteous gloom,
he was the only connection. What if the ambulance never
turned up? What if the medics couldn't see the guy on the
ground because the human traffic was too thick?

A sneeze shook him like a blow from a stranger. With
grudging steps he walked back to the guy on the ground,
who hadn't stirred. It occurred to Sam for the first time
that the guy might be dead. The thought hadn't entered
his head before. He panicked briefly. How odd that would
be, for such a dramatic thing not to show on a human
face, except by this discreet ribbon of blood and a certain
blueness about the lips. But Sam didn't believe it; these
things never happened to him or in his vicinity. He
thought maybe he should see if there was any sign of
warmth in the guy, but he couldn't decide which bit of
dirty raincoat to lay his hand on.

In case he wasn't dead, Sam should keep him warm,
yes, that was definitely to be recommended. Sam stared
around to see if there was a department store on the
block. He could buy a blanket, or one of those rugged tar-
tan picnic rugs. He would be willing to pay up to, say,
$100, considering the seriousness of the occasion; $125,
maybe, if that was what it took. But the only stores in
view sold lingerie, shoes, and smoked meats. He blew his
nose again.

Take off your coat, Sam told himself grimly. He did it, wincing as the cold air slid into his armpits. He was wearing a wool-blend suit, but it wasn't enough. This was probably a crazy idea, considering his own state of health.

He laid the Windsmoor over the man; it was stagy, like a gesture from some Shakespearean drama. No response yet. What if the warmth made the guy wake up, and Sam had to make conversation? No sign of life, nor death either. The coat lay too far up the guy's body, so it almost covered his head; it looked like the scene after a murder, Sam thought with a horrified inner giggle. He stooped again, took the coat by its deep hem, and dragged it delicately backward until it revealed the dirty white beard. Sam's keys slid out of a pocket and caught in a grating; he swooped to retrieve them. Jesus, imagine if he'd lost his keys on top of everything! Then he remembered his wallet and had to walk around the guy to reach the other pocket. Passersby might think he was picking the pockets of a dead man, like a scavenger on a battlefield.

He let out a spluttering cough. He could just feel his immune system failing. This cold would probably turn into something serious, like postviral fatigue or something. He should sit down and try some deep breathing. But where? The heating vent in front of him would be the warmest, but it would look so weird, a guy in an $800 suit squatting on the sidewalk beside a bum. But then, who did he think would be looking at him? he asked himself in miserable exasperation. And why should he care?

Sam let himself down on the curb at last. It was so cold on his buttocks, through the thin wool, it felt like he had wet himself. He stood up and kept moving, jigging on the spot. He couldn't remember the last time he'd been out in January without a winter coat. Like one of those squeegee punks who lived in layers of ragged sweaters. Was that snow, that speck in his eye, or just a cold speck of dust? He rubbed his leather-gloved hands against his cheeks. His sinuses were beginning to pulse.

Twice he heard a siren and began preparing his story—which sounded like a lie, in his head—and twice it turned out to be police, zooming by. After a quarter of an hour he no longer believed in the ambulance. His shoulders were going into tremors. For a moment he envied the guy on the vent, who looked almost cozy under the Windsmoor coat. He considered borrowing it back for a few minutes, just to get his core temperature up, but he was afraid of how it would look to passersby, and afraid to touch the guy again, besides. *The bum probably brought this on himself*, he thought very fast. *What goes around comes around. These people get what they deserve.*

Sam knew this was madness; he must be running a fever. He blew his nose again, though his handkerchief was a wet rag.

He felt a moment of pure temptation, melting sugar in his veins. All he had to do was pick up his coat, shake it off, put it on, and walk away.

He very nearly cried.

Thirty-two minutes according to his Rolex by the time the ambulance showed up. He wanted to be gruff with the paramedics but his voice came out craven with gratitude, especially when they said no, the guy wasn't dead yet. He begged them to let him climb into the ambulance after the stretcher. They seemed to think this was a sign of his concern, and reluctantly agreed, but the truth of the matter was that Sam was too cold to walk. He would have got into any heated vehicle, even with a psychopathic truck driver. Also there was the matter of his coat.

At the hospital the staff didn't tell him anything except to say that no, the guy wasn't dead. The doors of the ward flapped shut. The last thing Sam saw was his coat, draped over the end of the trolley. It occurred to him to ask for it back, but he couldn't think how to phrase it.

It turned out they really did call people John Doe, like in the movies. The forms were mostly blank, even after Sam and the receptionist had done their best. Sam was staggered by all the things he didn't know about the guy and couldn't begin to guess: *age, nationality, allergies.* He left his own name and address, and a little note about his coat, and set off walking to the subway. He was streaming from the eyes, the nose, the mouth, even. The dark night wrapped round him.

He knew he should feel better now. He had been a civic-minded citizen; committed what his scout leader had called a Good Deed for the Day; displayed what editorials termed *core Canadian values.* So why did he feel like shit?

"Bad day?" asked the owner of the corner shop as he sold Sam a carton of eggnog.

Was it written that plain on his face? Sam nodded

without a word. Only halfway down the street did it occur to him that, compared with nearly dying on the pavement, his day had been almost a pleasant one.

Sam waited till Monday before calling the hospital. He went down into the park to call, so no one from the office would get curious about his query. No, said the receptionist—a different one—she was not authorized to report on the condition of a patient except to a party named as the next of kin. Sam explained over and over again about John Doe not having any known kin. "I'm as near to kin as anyone else. You see, I'm . . ." But what was he? "I called about him, originally. I called 911," said Sam in a voice that sounded both boastful and ashamed.

The receptionist finally figured out which particular John Doe they were talking about. She relented enough to say that the patient had discharged himself that morning.

"What does that mean?"

"I'm not at liberty to say, sir."

Sam let the phone drop back into place. Guilt, again, like that twinge he felt whenever he went on the leg-curl machine at the gym. He should have visited the hospital yesterday. What would he have brought, though? Roses? Grapes? A bottle of meths? And what would he have said: *Here I am, your savior?*

Maybe in the back of his mind Sam had been thinking it would be like in the movies. An unexpected, heartwarming friendship of opposites; he would teach the street person to read, and in return would learn the wisdom of life in the rough. Who did he think he was kidding?

Sam went back to work with a poppy-seed bagel.

He got over his cold. He took up racquetball. He gave up on ever seeing his coat again, though he did keep one eye out for it on the various homeless guys downtown.

One evening during *This Hour Has 22 Minutes* Sam dimly remembered something from Sunday school about having two coats and giving away one. On a whim, he got up and opened his closet. Twenty-six coats and jackets. He counted them twice and he still couldn't believe it. He thought of giving away twenty-five of them. A dramatic gesture; faintly ludicrous, in fact. Which one would he keep, a coat to clothe and protect him in all seasons? Which one outer garment would say everything that had to be said about him? Which was the real Sam?

He shut the closet.

Always after that he thought of the whole thing as the Coat Episode—as if it had happened on *Seinfeld*. Ringing 911 was the one undeniably charitable thing he'd ever done face to face rather than through the barrier of a checkbook, and it made him cringe to remember. What good had he done? There was no such thing as saving someone's life. You couldn't make it easy to live or worth their effort. At most what you did was lengthen it by a day or a year, and hand it back to them to do the living.

At dinner parties, Sam liked to turn the petty happenings of his working day into funny stories. But never this one. Several times he found himself on the point of telling it—when the harshness of the winter came up as a topic, or provincial policy on housing—but he could never decide on the tone. He dreaded sounding pleased with himself, but he didn't want to beat his breast and have his friends console him, either.

What he would really have liked to tell them was his discovery: that it was all a matter of timing. If he'd been in the full of his health that day, he was sure he'd have risen grandly to the occasion. His courage would have been instant; his gestures, generous and unself-conscious. Then again, if he'd felt a fraction worse—if he'd discovered that he'd lost his handkerchief, say—he knew he'd have scurried on by. What Sam used to think of as his conscience—something solid, a clean pebble in his heart—turned out to depend entirely on the state of his nose.

Five weeks later the hospital sent his Windsmoor coat back in a plastic bag. It smelt harsh, as if it had been bleached. Sam hung it in his closet, but whenever it occurred to him to wear it, that winter, his hand skidded on by.

Finally he gave it to Goodwill, and bought a down jacket, like everybody else he knew.

The Sins of Salem

MARC ARONSON

*If ever there were witches, men and women in covenant with
the Devil, here are multitudes in New England.*

THE REVEREND SAMUEL PARRIS

Who Did This to You?

A child's screams pierce the black night lit only by stars.
Her mother races to her bed and her daughter sobs, say-
ing she feels as if her side is being stabbed with pins.
"Who, who did this to you?" the mother pleads.

This incident comes from a New England court record
dating from 1651, forty-one years before the famous Salem
witch trials, but if you listen carefully to the terrified
mother, you can understand exactly what took place four
decades later. Someone, in this case a child, is suffering.

Her mother assumes that the agonies must have a cause, and because she does not know about germs, or bacteria, or viruses, she immediately thinks of the agents she knows all too well: the Devil and his legion of allies.

Where do we look for causes, for blame, when someone we love is suffering? Though we have all been trained to call doctors and take pills, that is not always our first reaction. Instead we start with emotions that seem like sickness themselves: hatred, envy, jealousy, lust—the deadly sins. Is there something I have done wrong that has caused this pain, this punishment? Or, is there anyone who hates me or my child enough to cause this harm? We look for moral and emotional causes to explain physical experiences. The difference is that we don't say this out loud, instead we dole out aspirin and go to horror movies, pretending that the evil we secretly fear is safely up there on the screen.

In the seventeenth century stories of undead spirits, spell-casting wizards, dolls that could conduct the forces of evil were not merely private nightmares or public entertainments, they were how most doctors, judges, ministers, and average everyday people explained real life. In order to travel back in time to this mental world, just listen to your own thoughts late at night when the world seems eerie, and you are no longer so sure of the daylight logic of modern medicine. For our ancestors the figure who stood on the borderline between normal life and nightmare life was the witch.

According to both the law and popular belief, witches could be men *or* women. They could, on the surface, be the most devout of churchgoers, the most familiar of neighbors. But beneath these disguises they were not quite human anymore. In order to be able to use the Devil's powers—such as the ability to make a child feel pinpricks across her body, and even die—they had signed an unholy pact with the Devil himself: My soul for your dread power. Witches could use the dark emotions we still fear as weapons. This was a horrible sin. It was a kind of perversion of prayer. Even today a person might bargain with God—offering to give up a vice, promising to be generous to the needy, vowing to correct a wrong—to get divine help for a friend, to heal a child, to protect a soldier at war. But in the seventeenth century people asked an obvious question: If you can make deals with a good supernatural power, why not with an evil one?

A village afflicted with witchcraft was a terrifying place, for every person with a grudge, a grievance, a foul mouth was suspect. Running along the lines of malice, envy, pettiness that exist in every town were vile forces: a kind of evil electricity that could conduct harm and ruin lives. It was as if human failings opened tiny gaps in the fabric of the universe, and the dark liquor of evil could seep through them, fouling the town. Witchcraft explained why an innocent child could be suffering: look for a person who has had conflicts with the family, who envies the mother her child, the child her health, follow the lines of human hatred, and you are likely to find supernatural power. In reverse, then, find the hatred, find the cause of harm.

But how can you know for sure who is harboring hate,

stoking it, brooding on it, until he is so poisoned by it that he would make a dark pact to exact revenge? How can you know so certainly that you can go to the law and bring a court case? If you falsely accuse someone of witch-craft, isn't that also a sin? Isn't it possible that you, too, are weak, that your own fears and envies might allow you to see evil where there is none? Can we be sure when a per-son is actually wishing evil on us, or when it is only our own fear or guilt that has created a fantasy enemy? And even worse than that, once the family, the community, the town decides that there are agents of evil lurking in their midst, what is to prevent someone with a grudge from making a false accusation—calculating to do evil, under the guise of cleansing sin?

Who did this to you? How can I be sure? These were the questions that consumed Massachusetts in 1692; these were the questions that cost twenty-five people in Salem their lives (nineteen were hanged; five died in prison; one died when he refused to make a plea and, as was proper under English law, heavy stones were piled on his chest until he died). In the end, these were also the questions that ended the Salem trials and ensured that no witch would ever be convicted after that. And, yet, while we no longer have trials for witchcraft, we do have cases where fear, fear of Communists (as in the 1950s), fear of child abusers (as in the 1980s), of terrorists (as in the early years of the twenty-first century), creates panic. In each of these cases there were real evildoers, and, at least in the first two instances, there were also neighbors and friends who gave false or misguided testimony. A sin so horrible that sheer fear of it can induce new sins, that is a witch-hunt, and the classic case took place in Salem.

Who Believed in Witches?

Day by day in the Massachusetts of 1692, most people juggled and blended a variety of religious beliefs. In church and in their lengthy books and sermons, the most educated ministers warned people to trust only in God. Astrological predictions of the weather, "white magic" games that identified a girl's future husband, charms to identify or keep away witches were all considered wrong, for they used the Devil's powers. There was no such thing as dabbling in the occult. If you opened the door to evil, even a tiny crack, you risked your soul.

Puritans did not believe in the kind of prayer where a person makes an offer to sacrifice a vice or do a good deed in the hope that God will respond by granting his wishes. The godly, as they often called themselves, did not think a person could do anything at all to influence God: No amount of good deeds, sincere resolutions, hours spent in church could make the slightest bit of difference. The gap between God and humans was too vast to cross. You could pray. You might conduct a holy fast. You could discipline yourself to live by God's commandments. You might even hear the voice of God in your soul. But only if God chose to speak. Any effort to influence God, or guess His plans, was evil. Only the Devil bargained with people.

And yet, those same ministers—and nearly everyone else—constantly used charms and what we call "folk magic." Girls did crack eggs open into water to interpret the shapes as signs of whom they would marry. Women used roots and ceremonies to try to heal their children. Farmers tied special bags of herb concoctions to their animals when they pulled up lame. Even the ministers interpreted thunderclaps, hailstorms, strange sights in the sky as signs of God's judgments. No matter how often their official doctrines insisted that all power rested in God, people seemed to need rituals that told them that they, too, could do something to know the future or improve their lives.

In addition to high religion and folk belief many New Englanders also had a kind of savvy skepticism. Even though most people believed that witches were real, and witchcraft was a crime punishable by death, when the majority of cases came to court the judge or jury found the accused innocent or lessened the punishment. As in any small town, people knew enough about their neighbors to raise an eyebrow when a person who wanted land another owned suddenly discovered that the rival was a witch or to discount the ravings of a disturbed person who spoke of seeing the Devil. And there was also a small but growing and influential group of true rationalists who demanded scientific explanations of events and no longer believed in charms, folk magic, or witches at all.

And so, though accusations of witchcraft, campaigns against using the Devil's tools to predict the future, the bodies of convicted witches swinging from a hangman's noose (witches were never burned in North America) were all part of Puritan life in Massachusetts, they occurred more at the edges than the center—something like terrorism in America before September 11, 2001.

However, in the first few months of 1692, this jumble of beliefs fell out of balance. It was no longer possible to trust only in God but also check your astrological chart, to believe in witches and yet acquit those brought up for trial, to disbelieve in the occult and remain silent while accused witches were carted off to be executed.

Suddenly it seemed that all New England was afflicted by sin, but which one? Either a vile plague of witchcraft was taking place, a kind of otherworldly cancer that not only brought pain and suffering but also threatened the very existence of the colony dedicated to living by God's rules, or innocent people were being destroyed, and the religious faith that was the colony's reason for being was perversely turned into a killing machine. It would take nearly a year for New Englanders to decide which evil was consuming their lives, and the issue has continued to engage us throughout the rest of our still-unfolding history.

A Black Daylight Sky

If you could have seen the mental atmosphere of Salem in early 1692, it might have resembled the black, ominous, eerie quiet just before a summer hailstorm. Samuel Parris, a minister in Salem, certainly felt the charge in the air. The legion of hell, he warned, the foul enemy, was everywhere, and ever more dangerous. Get ready to fight, suspect all, and steel yourself to destroy. Week after week he preached fire, laboring to forge his congregation into an avenging arm of the Lord. But who was the enemy? Rich people, he asserted, greedy people, people who placed the hope of gain ahead of living pious lives. Covetousness, their selfish sin, was the open invitation to Satan. A person who put himself first, ahead of the tender care of his neighbors, who prospered in the world and then built a larger house, wore fancier clothes, maintained contacts with traders across the seven seas, was likely to be evil.

Strange thing about evil, though: Parris himself had set out to be just such a wealthy trader in Barbados but had failed. Only after making a muddle of business did he become a preacher. Only then did he turn the force of his bitter envy against the men who prospered where he had stumbled.

If some evil, some sin, was astir in Salem, was it greedy merchants who undermined and underpaid their ministers? There actually was a strong faction in the town of Salem that was growing wealthy through trade, a faction that did not like ministers such as Parris and did their best to hobble him. Or was it Parris himself, who used the Devil's brew of envy, hatred, and righteous anger in his congregation to get back at men he envied? Tension between worldly traders and Parris's stern farmers was rising in Salem, but this was just one of the gathering psychic storms.

New England for years had been fighting a real war with the native Wabanacki people in what is now Maine. Some of the victims of those conflicts were now living in Salem, working as servants for leading families, including Parris's strongest supporters.

These young women had watched their own parents and siblings being butchered before their eyes. Their dreams were haunted by nightmare images of bloody Indians. Most disturbing of all, they had heard terrifying and believable rumors that the murderous enemy had been secretly aided by important New Englanders, who had sold them guns or had traded their own safety for their neighbors' lives. As Parris mentally armed his congregation for war, young women with haunted eyes and nightmarish memories may have begun to feel that the evil they had fled was about to overtake them. And this time there would be no place to run. The traitorous allies of the satanic Indians might just be the most respected people in Salem, or even Boston.

The very first outbreak of strange symptoms in Salem, though, could have had an entirely different cause. Many people in Salem, including some teenagers and young women, were dabbling in using occult methods to learn about their futures. This was not unusual, nor particular to Salem. Four years earlier the children of a Boston family suffered horrible pains, seemed to fly, and went into wild fits in which they could not be dressed, fed, or taught. The Reverend Cotton Mather claimed to have healed them through a combination of prayer, close and caring observation, and exposing the mother of their laundress as a witch. She was duly convicted and executed by the courts. Mather wrote up the case history, and then he and other ministers used the story as a warning about the reality of witchcraft and the danger of toying with the Devil.

Sometime—probably in January of 1692—Reverend

Parris's daughter and his niece began to act in strange ways reminiscent of people under demonic attack. Were Abigail Williams (aged eleven or twelve, we are not sure) and Elizabeth (Betty) Parris (who was nine) suffering from the same afflictions as the children in Boston? If so, there must be a witch nearby. But from the very first a skeptic named Robert Calef raised another possibility: overimaginative, silly, theatrical young people could be imitating behaviors they had read about. Mather's warnings could also serve as an instruction manual: If you want people to think witches are attacking you, or even if you just want to have some fun and get away with it, behave in such and such a way.

Salem was filled almost to overflowing with inner tensions. But it took one more spark for it to explode, and that was related to a sin only modern people would recognize as such.

Like many New England families, Parris had a servant, a slave named Tituba, who had been born in Barbados. All evidence suggests that Tituba was an Indian herself, brought as a slave to the island from North America, or more likely from the area that is now Venezuela and Guyana. A neighbor pressured her and her husband, John Indian, or perhaps just John alone, to try a bit of English ritual magic. The neighbor insisted that they bake some of the Parris girls' urine into a rye cake and feed it to a dog. The animal would then lead them to the witch who was afflicting them.

The cake was baked, and the test performed. Suddenly a witch was exposed—it was Tituba herself! By the logic of the ministers, this should not have mattered at all. As Parris said, employing a folk magic test was "going to the Devil for help against the Devil." It was no less demonic than a love charm or an astrological chart, and no more likely to be accurate. As many of the accused witches in Salem would soon point out, the Devil could lie about who was a witch just as easily as he could lie in his promises of wealth, power, or revenge. But for some reason both theology and rationality were suspended, and Tituba as well as two other suspected witches was brought to trial.

With modern eyes we might suspect that her status as an Indian slave made Tituba an easy scapegoat. But that is not how it worked out. As a slave she must have had a lifetime's experience in saying whatever would please her masters in order to avoid blame. While the other two accused witches protested their innocence—which made the court see them as all the more dangerous and unrepentant—Tituba quickly grasped that the way to save herself was to admit being a witch, and to feed the court lurid details of a hellish plot. She revealed that the two afflicted girls, and the three witches, were just the first signs of a sinister conspiracy involving at least nine witches in both Salem and Boston, monstrous creatures and familiars, and a man in black, who seemed very much like the Devil himself. After she told her vivid tale, Tituba was jailed, but also ignored. Though her story opened the door to the witch-hunt that followed, she survived all of the trials.

But why did the judges trust first a demonic test, and then the elaborate fantasies of an accused witch? Why could they not listen to the doubts raised both by believers who didn't accept the Devil's tests and skeptics who dismissed the "antics" of the afflicted young women? Yet another sin may hold the key to this mystery.

Many of the men who were appointed to conduct the trials in Salem turned out to be the people who had reason to fear blame for the lives lost in the campaigns against the Indians. Their competency as military commanders, their skill as diplomats, even their loyalty to New England had come under question. Now they were hearing that another sort of attack was under way—a demonic invasion. How appealing—instead of being subject to censure, they could be relentless scourges; instead of fearing condemnation, they could mete out punishment; instead of reckoning with their human failings, they could combat supernatural enemies. We have no way of knowing if the judges consciously chose to shift blame or were just emotionally ready to be swept up in the accusations, but swept up they were.

What a lineup of sins: merchants eager to undermine a minister who criticized them; the fire-breathing preacher out to condemn those he could not match in business skill; terrified young women interpreting new events through the scrim of past horrors; ministers feeling their authority weakening, and publicizing stories of possession and witchcraft to prove their worth; young people dabbling in the occult and either experiencing or faking symptoms of demonic affliction; a slave spinning stories to save her life; and judges only too eager to believe the worst so that they could remain above suspicion themselves. And yet it took one last sin for this alignment of evils to change from a brief outbreak into a witch-hunt, and that, some historians believe, was the simple sin of falsehood.

Come, Join the Evil Band

You hear rumors: You've been named; they are after you. You know yourself to be innocent; you have nothing to hide, nothing to worry about. But the rumors get louder: You are next. A knock at the door, "Report to court, you are accused of being a witch." You open the door of the plain, wooden, meeting hall and take your seat. From the second you arrive, the wailing begins. One screams, another yells that you, your evil spirit, is biting her—she waves her arm at the judge, insisting that he examine it to see the exact prints of your teeth. You glance over and people start choking at your gaze, as if you could beam out invisible rays that burned the air.

"I am innocent," you protest. But then an accuser jumps up and points above your head: "There it is, I can see it, the evil bird that does her bidding." "Yes, yes, I see it too," another says. "Look, now, she's cutting herself with a pin to feed it." "Grab the pin, get it," a third screams.

The more you resist the howling mob, the angrier they become. Desperate to escape, you suddenly remember something you've noticed: All of those who have been hanged denied being witches, while those who have confessed are jailed and ignored. "Perhaps I did see the Devil," you start to say. "When, where, who was he with?" asks the judge, but the crowd is calmer now, almost soothing, encouraging you along this safe, new path. "Yes, I did. I am sorry for my lies. I am a witch." Your accusers look upon you with kindness; you have made the right choice and joined them.

This pattern would take place over and over again during the hearings. How could the accusers have had so much control—to faint on cue, to demand having their limbs examined, to even produce pins in court—unless they had planned it? And if they had, if they consciously created a courtroom machine that turned innocent people into confessors, why? It is one thing to say the accusers were haunted girls who believed their neighbors were evil, or that whatever their initial motivation, once the trials began they felt they were in too deep and could not stop their accusations. It is another to claim that they crafted their performances, and yet there is a great deal of evidence that they did just that.

One of the most active accusers was Ann Putnam, Jr. Years later, after the trials had long ended, she made a confession of her own. She wrote out a statement, handed it to her minister, and asked him to read it to the congregation. Ann admitted that she had been an "instrument for the accusing of several persons of a grievous crime, whereby their lives were taken away from them." If Putnam was an instrument, who or what was pulling the strings? She did not say. Instead, Ann claimed that it was Satan who had deluded her. That leaves it to us to guess which humans might have controlled her actions.

It is possible that Ann was the instrument of some group that plotted to use the trials for their own ends.

After all, her own family strongly supported Reverend Parris and detested the rising merchants. Could they have put her up to the whole show? Possibly. Mercy Lewis, one of the young women who may have been traumatized by the Indian wars, was a servant in the Putnam family household. Could she have terrorized and manipulated Ann into being her performing puppet? Maybe. For whatever reason Ann, and probably others, seem likely to have put on deadly shows in court.

Horror of Conscience

Sin after sin after sin, kept spinning along by lies—that was the pattern of the Salem trials. But then, amidst all the horrors, another voice began to be heard. Young women who had confessed to being witches, who had sent others to be hanged, but who were now safely out of sight of the judges and liars, recanted. "I was in such horror of conscience that I could not sleep for fear the Devil should carry me away for telling such horrid lies," admitted Margaret Jacobs. She took back the accusations that had cost her grandfather his life.

Once confessed witches began to risk their lives to speak the truth, the powerful machinery of accusation and blame began to crack. The most telling blow came from an accused woman who refused to take the easy road of confession and false accusation. Mary Easty begged the court to reexamine its rules, to question the accusers one by one, so that they could not operate together as a pack. The judges did not listen, so she sent them a final message: "I petition to your honors not for my own life for I know I must die and my appointed time is set but . . . if it be possible no more innocent blood may be shed." She spoke with a perfectly Christian acceptance of her fate, and willingness to die, if it would help others.

In the end, Salem is an almost biblical story: People were accused of selling their souls, but in the end it was conscience, the voice of the soul, that triumphed. Once the trials began, the easiest, safest thing for the accused to do was to sin, to lie. You didn't even have to tell a very harmful lie—the court did not mind if you only accused people who were already dead. Even that paltry confession gave you the temporary safety of going to jail. But some people could not stand to lie or to keep telling the same falsities over and over. Some were even ready to die, if they might save others. As the recantations mounted, and the skeptics grew more vocal in their protests, the leading ministers of the land took notice. Cotton Mather's father, Increase, perhaps the most important minister in New England, finally said, "It were better that ten suspected witches should escape, than that one innocent person should be condemned." With that, the power of the theatrical accusers, the defensive judges, the angry Reverend Parris was broken.

In Salem the language of blame—who harmed my child; it must be a witch—came to rule a community. But in Salem, too, the language of conscience—I cannot lie, even at the cost of my life—eventually triumphed. That is an example of human behavior that is as powerful, and as inspiring, today as it was in 1692.

Excerpt from

Leatherstone

DAVID PABIAN

Jasper Leatherstone had escaped. A dragnet was out for him, its dogs howling through the night. At the edge of a frozen river he could hear them coming and took a chance only the most desperate or insane would. With superhuman strength he hurled a boulder through the ice and plunged in after it. His body shocked past feeling by the cold, he swam like some polar animal under the ice, and when his lungs gave out he took a knife he'd stolen and broke through the underside to gulp down frozen air. But the current grabbed him and tore him downstream, battering him on rocks, dragging him to the bottom, flinging him up to crack his head on the ice ceiling and slamming him against the massive root of a tree. He pulled himself along it, though the current did its best to tear him away. Smashing his fists through the ice at the shore, he drove the knife into the tree, pulled himself through the jagged ice break, and fell on the black earth, twisting and hissing like a reptile. When the police and dogs got to the river three miles back, the trail was lost.

• I •

It was 1959, the year I was twelve, when it all happened. My name's John Garrett, but I'm called Champ. My dad had conferred the tag on me at the beginning of my existence, probably when he was told the undersized seven-week-preemie in the incubator was his son. It must have been a moment of sublimely hopeless hopefulness for him. And I grew up never failing to experience a pang of guilt at the sound of my name. John's a neutral name, conjuring up no image at all. But Champ's a name redolent of images and implications I knew I'd never live up to.

If the wrong side of the tracks had a wrong side, that's where we lived—myself, my sister, Lizzie, our uncle Caleb, and Dad, when he was around. He was usually on the road, though, struggling to sell tools to mom-and-pop hardware stores about to go under. The chain outfits were starting up in a big way then, and they had their own buyers off in urban high-rises where they were ignorant of life in small towns like ours. But Dad kept at it, making just enough to keep us in food and clothes and a little spending money, and occasionally he even came home for a couple of weeks. Things were different when he was there, more joyful, more fun, because he never seemed to take anything too seriously, especially himself. But sooner or later he'd have to hit the road again.

Lizzie was seventeen and kind of pretty, with her brownish gold hair and large, sad eyes that always seemed to be focused inward, no matter what she was looking at. For the most part, she inhabited her own private world, a world I couldn't really understand or even imagine, because she was what they used to call "slow."

As for Uncle Caleb, he lived mostly in the Trophy Room, the bar at Horizon Lanes, a bowling alley in Horizon Village, the big development over on the right side of the tracks. He claimed the Trophy Room made the best cocktails in the state. He always called liquor *cocktails,* no matter what form it came in, and always tried to sound gentlemanly and refined when he said the word.

We lived in an old wood-frame house at the edge of the woods about a mile and a half outside Horizon Village, so we weren't considered real "Villagers," even though my dad's family had settled there long before the town was built. Almost all the other kids at school lived in town. I was the hick whose dad was too dumb to move off the farm and into a nice new tract home like everyone else had done; the hick whose dad drove a ten-year-old car; the hick whose dad looked down on all the hardworking inhabitants of the new modern development of comfortable, modular homes; the hick with the "reetard" sister and the "wino" uncle; the hick who never played in Little League, who never played anything because he didn't like sports (and that made the hick a sissy Communist hick on top of all his other hickness).

I was also considered a geek because I had an interest in science, although I didn't apply myself to it particularly well at school. The experiments we conducted in class—growing mold in petri dishes, desalinizing a glass of salt water—weren't dramatic enough for me. I wanted lightning, thunder, explosions, lights all over town killed by the incredible experiments going on in the mysterious old laboratory on the hill, like in the science fiction and horror movies we saw on Saturdays at the Horizon Theater. They featured laboratories crammed with amazing equipment—bubbling vials, jars full of obscure specimens, and cages crawling with god knows what. I especially loved the Frankenstein movies, even the really terrible ones like *Frankenstein's Daughter* and *I Was a Teenage Frankenstein*.

The one that started it, though, the first Frankenstein movie, remained a mystery to me. It was too old for the Horizon Theater to show, it hadn't yet turned up on television in our area, and of course, there was no such thing as home video then. I wondered how it all began, who the first monster was and why he was created. As smart as I thought I was, it never occurred to me to go to the library and check out the original novel by Mary Shelley.

It was my fascination with these cheesy films that the other guys found so funny, so geeky and nerdy. I loved the laboratory apparatuses in them, and tried to figure out what everything did and how it was all connected. Part of me knew I was just looking at a movie set, but another part of me was thinking that all the scientific paraphernalia up there was somehow logically designed and really worked. You could see the electricity jumping and crackling between the coils, hear the fluids bubbling in the jars.

Why would they go to all the trouble of hooking it up if it couldn't really do something?

· II ·

The original *Frankenstein* finally showed up on our local TV station. It was the night my mother died. My dad got a call from the hospital where she'd been for two weeks and ran out of the house without saying a word. I knew there was trouble, but this had happened before and I was sure they'd stabilize her and he'd come home to tell us, again, that she'd be all right, no matter what all the doctors said.

The movie was made in 1931 and was old and strange and alien to me, nothing like the horror movies we saw at the Horizon Theater. The monsters in those were usually unleashed by an atom bomb or came from outer space, and were generally so lacking in human characteristics that they weren't very scary. But this Frankenstein creation was something else. He was inhuman and soulless, yet at the same time *very* human: as sad-eyed as Lizzie, he moved jerkily, spasmodically, and—covered with terrible scars—was the ultimate outcast. But Frankenstein, the man who made him, said something in the movie that set my mind spinning. He said he had discovered "the great ray that first brought life into the world." He meant a new light ray, a source of power unknown till then. Well, that light ray struck my imagination. Light and electricity, things I'd taken for granted and had never really given much thought to as a source of true power, were suddenly exciting and magical to me. Then in the movie, Frankenstein got all his electrical gear going, and in the most amazing movie laboratory sequence I'd ever seen, sent the man he'd put together up into a lightning storm and brought him to life. I'll never forget seeing that scarred hand with those dead black nails trembling into animation. But things soon started going all to hell and the monster took off on a killing spree.

We didn't get to finish the movie because about ten minutes before it ended, Dad came home and told us Mom was dead. The TV was still on and I could hear the monster screaming while it died, and I wanted to look at the set and watch, but I didn't.

A week later, the day after the funeral, another Frankenstein movie was on and the monster was still alive. He was indestructible, someone in the movie said. And apparently he was, because our local channel showed a different Frankenstein movie each week for about five weeks. Some of them were pretty good, most were terrible, but that wasn't the point—it was the *idea* of the monster, assembled from dead men and electrified into life again and again, that fascinated me. It seemed like such a simple idea; why couldn't it be done? The more I thought about it, the more obsessed I became with the idea of being able to bring something dead back to life with electricity. It was exactly the sort of scientific experiment I'd been itching to do. And since I hadn't ever seen anything about it in *Popular Science,* one of my favorite magazines, and the idea had never been disproved as far as I knew, I figured I'd be treading new ground, a pioneer. And *I* wouldn't make the same mistake Frankenstein had made.

His creature was a monster because he'd mistakenly put a criminal brain into its head. Well, I knew I wouldn't be manufacturing any sort of human being, I just wanted to see if I could revive something already dead, maybe a body from the morgue—skipping for the moment how I'd get away with that.

I didn't tell anyone my big idea yet, because I didn't want to hear that it was impossible or stupid or that I was crazy. I needed to think about it for a while and try to figure out a practical way of accomplishing it. So I stayed quiet, watched after Lizzie, and tried not to make things any harder for my dad.

My mom's death had left him a wreck. He'd always been kind of a loner, and, like me, hadn't ever really fit in. Mom had told him he was someone special, though, and had made him feel that way, too. Now that she was gone, I'd catch him looking around the place, at the repairs that needed to be made, at the overgrown yard he'd never been interested in keeping up; he'd look and look until he'd finally just slump into a chair in defeat. When he lost Mom, he lost his anchor and suddenly seemed to be drifting aimlessly.

And now we were running out of money and he was going to have to hit the road again. He said he didn't want to leave us, had even checked out a couple of local places for work, but there just wasn't anything, and anyway, all he really knew was selling. That's when Uncle Caleb, mom's brother, offered to stay with us—temporarily, "until something local turns up for you," he said to Dad. At first Dad was dubious because we all knew Uncle Caleb drank too much.

"C'mon, Mike," he protested (Mike was my dad's name), "I've turned over a new leaf. When was the last time you saw me with a cocktail?"

"You had some wine after the funeral," Dad said. "A lot."

"Well, sure, it was a funeral," Uncle Caleb whined. "But I've really cut back. And, of course, if I was watching the kids I wouldn't drink at all. It's no big deal, I've always been able to take it or leave it."

Not knowing anything about alcohol addiction, and not having any other options anyway, Dad took him at his word and agreed to let him stay. "Temporarily," he reminded him, "just until something local turns up for me."

That's when Uncle Caleb came to live with us, and it soon became obvious that he hadn't turned over any new leaves, and had never bothered to look up the meaning of the word *temporary*. But when Dad was on the road and I talked with him on the phone, I didn't say anything about Uncle Caleb's drinking or behavior. Dad had been so miserable when Mom died, and now that he was back at work and doing what he enjoyed, I didn't want to make him worry. Besides, we needed the money. If he felt he had to come home and couldn't find work, we'd be in real trouble. I figured Uncle Caleb's moods were a small price to pay for Dad's peace of mind.

• • •

So that was my life, and that's when I started reading up on electricity, positive that it would be a simple thing to use it to turn death back into life. But I couldn't find anything on electrical resurrection at all, which puzzled me at first, until it dawned on me that it was probably because of some religious beliefs or something; that trying to reanimate dead matter was considered a "sinful" act by those inclined to such beliefs. Well, I wouldn't have any problem with that, because I wasn't religious. Dad said you had to believe in yourself, not in some old gray-bearded geezer in a fairy-tale land called Heaven.

After some months of mulling it over and still not being sure of how to implement my plan, I finally broke down and told Ken and Jeff about it. They were two years older than me and normally I would have been afraid to say "boo" to them, especially Ken, since he was one of the most popular kids in school. That made him cocky, and he strutted around like a god, but his dad was an electrician, and I was desperate. Jeff was let in by default, since he worshipped at the altar of Ken and stuck to him like some kind of holy adhesive.

"You want to do what?" Ken asked incredulously. "Bring some dead guy back to life?"

"That's wrong. It's . . . it's a sin."

That was Jeff, taking his cue from Ken's reaction.

"You sound like a friggin' Catholic," Ken scoffed at him. "Sin! Just exactly what does that mean, anyways?"

Jeff hated being ridiculed by Ken. "Well, you know." He squirmed. "When you do something bad. Something, like, against God. Or something."

"So, what's so bad about what we're gonna do?" Ken challenged him.

"It's playing God." Jeff was weakening, unsure of his argument in the face of Ken's self-assurance. "If you bring something dead back to life, that's playing God."

"We're experimenting here," Ken explained with exaggerated patience. "God wants us to learn all we can about stuff—that's why he gave us brains."

"Sure, I know that, but . . . even in the movie, Dr. Frankenstein thought that what he did was a sin, that it was wrong." Jeff looked tortured. The last thing he wanted was to look uncool in Ken's eyes.

"No he didn't; he even got the girl." And that settled that, at least for Ken, who turned back to me.

"I'll tell you what, doofus, you give me all the beer I want and I'll help you do this. Otherwise, forget it."

"Beer? Where am I supposed to get beer?"

"You could tap your uncle's jugular—that's pretty much all he's got in his veins."

He looked at Jeff for approval and got it in a big laugh and a thumbs-up sign.

I studied him as I considered his proposal, wondering why he was so damn commanding and why I felt so cowed by him.

"Well, I could maybe get a couple every so often," I finally said weakly, thinking of the stacks of Uncle Caleb's six-packs in the refrigerator, and how he was usually too drunk to keep count of them.

"I knew you wouldn't disappoint me." Ken grinned with that lopsided grin that always got the girls. Then, when he just stood there looking at me, I realized our arrangement had already gone into effect and went down into the house and brought him back a six-pack.

"Now listen," he said after finishing one can and starting on another. "Theoretically this idea of yours should work. If you can shock a body into death, you should be able to shock it into life—we're basically all just a bunch of electrical impulses, anyway. But we'll need a complete body. We can't make one. Any idiot knows that."

I didn't like the way he looked at me when he said that, so I challenged him. "Knows what?"

"That you can't put a body together like they did in the movies. The parts would all reject each other."

"I know that," I lied. Actually, I'd never heard about foreign body parts rejecting each other. "Maybe we can steal a body from the morgue or something."

"You're creeping me out, kid. We're not going to start that way. For now we'll go with animals. Dead animals are always easy to find. Maybe later we can move on to the big stuff. Now, we need a car battery. Can you get one?"

Sure I could. That night I broke into Taylor's Hardware and stole a tractor battery. I had no problem with stealing back then; I just figured that if I couldn't afford something—and I could *never* afford anything—I'd just steal it. I knew stealing was wrong, my parents had told me it was, but I knew it only in an intellectual way. I didn't connect then with the human aspect of stealing; how it affects the people you steal from. Although my dad was never a thief, he was a nonconformist, and it was easy for me to justify my petty larcenies as just bucking the status quo, a trait he

upheld as a sign of true individualism. It made me feel like
Robin Hood, stealing from the rich to give to the poor—
except "the poor" was only me.

We had a barn on our property we never used. My
grandparents had converted its loft into a makeshift
apartment with the idea of renting it out. For a kitchen it
had a hot plate and an ancient refrigerator, and it had a
sort of bathroom fitted out with a sink, toilet, and shower.
To run the shower you had to hook a hose to the sink and
then everything ran down an outside pipe into a big
cesspool. It never did rent, but I slept there sometimes
when I needed to get out of the house. Up there I couldn't
hear Uncle Caleb yelling and falling over stuff, and I
could fall asleep on Grandpa's old army cot. Now the loft
became our laboratory and Ken rigged up the stolen battery to an old generator that had been hooked to an abandoned trailer in his yard. I lifted some jumper cables from
Horizon Gas and Garage to conduct the life charge
through our monster, whatever, or whoever, it finally
turned out to be.

Ken self-importantly informed us that physical stimu-
lation by electricity was galvanization, so we called our
monster-making machine the Galvanizer.

We started small. Jeff caught one of the wild chickens
that had been living in the brush off the highway ever
since a poultry truck had flipped over and broken up
there a few years back. He wrung its neck, then attached
the jumper cables to its feet and beak and cranked up the
generator. At first it squawked and flopped around, but
then it started cooking and smelled awful, what with its

feathers and all, nothing like a prepared roasting fowl, so we had to trash it. We caught a few more chickens, killed them and tried to bring them back, but we never could.

"I figure it's because we wrung their necks," Ken said.

"I bet you're right," said Jeff, who always bet Ken was right. "If you break someone's neck to kill him you'd have to fix that first before you could bring him back. We should've thought of that."

"*I* thought of it." Ken smirked. "I knew it wouldn't work; I just wanted to show you two morons that it wouldn't."

Even Jeff rolled his eyes at that. Fortunately for him, Ken was chugging the last of his beer and didn't notice.

"I'm empty," he announced, crushing his Schlitz can and tossing it across the room. He checked the refrigerator and seeing no beer, ordered, "Go get some more from the house, squirt."

"Get it yourself," I said, tired of his superiority, "and don't call me squirt."

I figured he'd kill me for that, but my life was saved when we heard Uncle Caleb's car drive up. Even its engine sounded drunk, and Ken and Jeff took off to avoid having to exchange pleasantries with him. I went down to the house and prepared for another cozy evening with the family.

My two partners in crime stopped coming around soon after that. Maybe it was the fact that we hadn't revived any dead animals and Ken was starting to look stupid, maybe it was just that he'd found another beer source, or maybe it was just too hard to get out to our place—because at the beginning of November, we were hit by a cold front, the worst in a century. It was from Canada, but if you had told me it came from the North Pole, I'd have believed you. We got something like ten feet of snow in three days. The river froze over, then the schools were closed, and Dad, who'd planned to come home, couldn't because the roads were blocked. When the constant snowing finally stopped and the schools reopened, I had gotten used to not going, so I didn't. I made sure Lizzie went back, though—she was in a class with other "special" kids, and was driven there every morning by the mother of one of her classmates. Then I'd go out to the barn and wait for Uncle Caleb to leave. As soon as he was gone, I'd hop on my bike and do whatever I wanted with my day.

And that's how it happened that on one of those aimless days I found my monster in the dark, tangled woods, and my life changed forever.

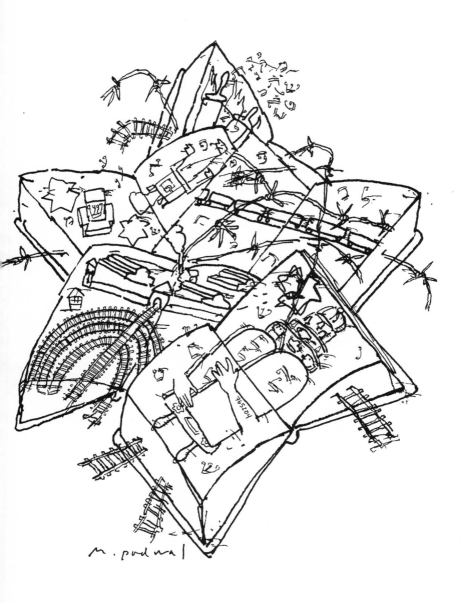

Pages of Persecution   MARK PODWAL

What Would I Have Done?

HAZEL ROCHMAN

Nearly six million Jews in Europe were murdered by Hitler and Nazi Germany, deliberately and systematically, only because they were Jews. About five million gentile civilians were also killed, including Romani, gays, the disabled, Jehovah's Witnesses, Russians, Polish Catholics, and political prisoners.

How could the Holocaust happen? Who is guilty? Could it happen again? Could it have happened to my friend? To me? What would I have done? More than half a century after the end of World War II, survivors, writers, and artists continue to ask these questions with haunting intensity.

I am Jewish, and an awareness of the Holocaust is part of my history. During World War II, while I was growing up in a big extended immigrant family in Johannesburg,

South Africa, the Holocaust seemed very close, my worst nightmares come true. What if "they" suddenly invaded my comfortable home and dragged me and my parents away? My grandparents had left Eastern Europe around 1910 to escape hard times and anti-Semitism. My father was three years old. Some of my relatives went to America, but my grandparents traveled steerage on a boat to South Africa. Some relatives stayed behind in the Old Country. During the Holocaust, my husband's grandmother and aunt were herded by the Nazis into the Vilna Ghetto, where they died. One uncle was shot to death. Another has never been heard from. When a third uncle returned to his home in Poland after the war, he was chased out by the new owners.

During WWII when I was a child, the major opposition party in South Africa was pro-Nazi. Some of our neighbors told my father that Jewish blood would run in the streets. He made secret arrangements to hide me with a gentile family if the anti-Semites gained power. In fact, the pro-Nazis did become the government after the war, and they made racism the law. But the people they persecuted were not the Jews, but the blacks. It took me a long time to realize that my nightmares were happening to the people around me.

They called this racism apartheid (pronounced "a-part-hate"), which is Afrikaans for apartness, or separate development. There was no deliberate genocide, but hunger, prison, family separation, torture, murder, and exile were common experiences. Apartheid was sanctified by the Dutch Reformed Church. The whites told themselves they had a divine mission to care for the "inferior" blacks and to defend racial purity against "barbarism." The law made Africans foreigners in their own country. If you were black, you had to carry a pass, a document that showed you had permission to work in a white area, and you had to produce your pass for any policeman.

And that word "homeland" that we're now hearing here all the time has ugly associations for me. The apartheid government used "homeland" to mean exactly the opposite of home. Although black people made up more than three-quarters of the population, they were given about thirteen percent of the land. People saw bull-dozers come into their communities and destroy their houses, and thousands were forcibly "relocated," dumped in places they'd never seen; they were told these barren places were their "homelands." That was the official word. Another word for those places was reserves or reservations. And everyone in a homeland was the same, accord-ing to the racist authorities.

This is how Mark Mathabane describes a police raid on his home and neighborhood in *Kaffir Boy: The True Story of a Black Youth's Coming of Age in Apartheid South Africa* (1986): "A huge throng of handcuffed black men and women, numbering in the hundreds, filled the nar-row streets from side to side. The multitude, murmuring like herds of restless cattle, was being marched by scores of black policemen and a dozen or so white ones, some of whom had fierce police dogs on leashes, toward a row of about ten police vans and trucks parked further down the street. More handcuffed men and women were still filing out of the yards on either side, swelling the ranks of those already choking the streets. It seemed as if the entire population of Alexandra had been arrested."

That scene in Alexandra was happening barely five miles from the comfortable home where I was growing up on a tree-lined Johannesburg street. Did I know about what was happening to Mark Mathabane's family? Well, not really. Oh yes, I was against apartheid. But police raids had nothing to do with me. I was a bystander. I did nothing. For a long time.

In his autobiography, *Long Walk to Freedom* (1994), Nelson Mandela describes what it was like for black people under apartheid oppression: "It was a crime to walk through a Whites Only door, a crime to ride a Whites Only bus, a crime to use a Whites Only drinking fountain, a crime to walk on a Whites Only beach, a crime to be on the streets past eleven, a crime not to have a pass book, and a crime to have the wrong signature in that book, a crime to be unemployed and a crime to be employed in the wrong place, a crime to live in certain places and a crime to have no place to live."

It took me a long time to realize that those crimes were part of the daily life around me.

That's why I think it's important to connect the Holocaust history with racism through history and right now, from slavery to apartheid to ethnic cleansing.

The Holocaust was not unique. Of course, if we say that every form of cruelty and racism is a holocaust, that does lessen the enormity of what Hitler called his "Final Solution." But there can be no hierarchy of suffering.

Millions of non-Jews in Europe died for their opposition to Nazism. And mass persecution did not begin or end with the Nazis. Extreme as the Nazi genocide was, it was not a thing apart. It was human experience. As camp survivor Bruno Bettelheim said, it was what ordinary people did to ordinary people.

Primo Levi in *Survival in Auschwitz* (1959), his stark account of the ten months he spent in the Nazi death camp, imagines how he and the other Jewish prisoners must appear to the civilians as "untouchables": "They think, more or less explicitly ... that as we have been condemned to this life of ours, reduced to our condition, we must be tainted by some mysterious, grave sin. They hear us speak in many different languages, which they do not understand, and which sound to them as grotesque as animal noises; they see us reduced to ignoble slavery, without hair, without honor and without names, beaten every day, more abject every day, and they never see in our eyes a light of rebellion, or of peace, or of faith. They know us as thieves and untrustworthy, muddy, ragged, and starving, and mistaking the effect for the cause, they judge us worthy of our abasement."

The blame-the-victim racism he describes is startlingly familiar today and so is the terminology. Whether in South Africa or Germany or the U.S., people use the same clichés. The objects of revulsion always seem to speak in grotesque-sounding foreign languages; they deserve what they get because they are lazy, dirty, and physically disgusting; and they are nameless.

Slavery is an abomination that has affected millions. In

From Slave Ship to Freedom Road (1998), Rod Brown's stirring narrative paintings show the history of slavery through dramatic group scenarios: the horror of capture, the voyage over, the auction, the labor, and also the secret bonds of community and defiance on the plantation and on the Underground Railroad. The pictures, with Julius Lester's impassioned commentary, make us imagine the daily life in the cabin, in the fields, and in the house; the importance of storytelling, of religion; the anguish when a child is sold away. In contrast, Brown shows the horrifying impersonality of the slave ships, the bodies stacked head to foot on bunks. It could be a scene from Auschwitz.

Many American Indian nations were decimated as Europeans colonized the Americas. In *When Plague Strikes* (1995), James Cross Giblin describes the deliberate strategy of British commander Sir Jeffrey Amherst to infect the Native Americans with smallpox. In letters to one of his colonels in 1763, he wrote: "Could we not contrive to send the smallpox among these... tribes of Indians? We must use every stratagem in our power to reduce them.... You will do well to try to infect the Indians by means of blankets, as to try every other method that can serve to extirpate this execrable race."

In 1915 the Turkish government massacred as many as one and a half million Armenians. Adam Bagdasarian's novel *Forgotten Fire* (2000) is based on the experience of his great-uncle fleeing the genocide. On the frontispiece, Bagdasarian quotes Hitler: "Who does now remember the Armenians?"

In Cambodia in the 1970s about two million people

died at the hands of the Khmer Rouge Communists. And ethnic cleansing is still a threat in many parts of the world. Samantha Power is founding director of the Carr Center for Human Rights at the John F. Kennedy School of Government at Harvard University. In her book *A Problem from Hell: America and the Age of Genocide,* for which she won a Pulitzer Prize and the 2003 National Book Critics Circle Award for nonfiction, she speaks with passion and insight about U.S. foreign policy in the twentieth century, including not only the Holocaust but also our nation's more recent policies in Cambodia, Rwanda, and Bosnia. She asks key questions about our role as bystander ("Why does the United States stand so idly by?") and also talks about people who tried to make a difference.

The eloquent Palestinian spokesperson Hanan Ashrawi, in her autobiography, *This Side of Peace* (1995), uses a powerful phrase. She says there's no "upmanship" of suffering, no monopoly of pain, among Jews and Palestinians. There is racism from all sides in the Middle East today. The Israeli writer Amos Oz in an amazing interview on the PBS *NewsHour* (1/23/02) said that what he wants to show in his fiction is that "deep down all our secrets are the same . . . somewhere beyond race and religion and ideology and all the other great dividers, the insecure, timid, craving, and trembling self is very often very close to the next insecure, timid, craving, hoping, fearing, terrified self . . . even on the slopes of an erupting volcano, there still may be everyday life. There still may be loneliness and longing and death and desolation. These are the everlasting materials of life."

In her poetry collection *19 Varieties of Gazelle* (2002), Palestinian American writer Naomi Shihab Nye writes about the Middle East and about being Arab American. The book was a finalist for the National Book Award. Her introduction was written in the wake of September 11 and in it she says that poetry cherishes the small details that a large disaster erases. Her best poems combine the two, the small details and the big disasters, what happens to young people when bombs fall where they live. And she sounds like Amos Oz when she says, "I'm not interested in / who suffered the most / I'm interested in / people getting over it."

What about *Anne Frank: The Diary of a Young Girl?*

If you've read nothing else about the Holocaust, you've probably read this.

Translated from the Dutch, it's a classic journal, kept by a Jewish teenager during the two years, from 1942 to 1944, that she, her family, and several others hid from the Nazis in a secret annex in Amsterdam, Holland. Since it was first published in 1947, the diary has sold more than twenty-five million copies in fifty languages. In 1995 a new definitive edition was published, which restored diary entries that were left out of the first edition, including Anne's interest in her Jewishness and in her sexuality.

Yet the diary is the subject of a growing attack for the very things that make it so popular: because it is hopeful and because Anne Frank is just an ordinary kid like many of her readers. Cynthia Ozick in the *New Yorker* (10/6/97) writes a devastating attack, not on the diary but on how it has been exploited from the time it was first published. And she shows that the attempt to make Anne a generic teenager distorts the truth and transforms her Holocaust story into a sweetly upbeat coming-of-age novel. That famous sentence, "Still I believe, in spite of everything, that people are really good at heart," has been wrenched out of context and trumpeted on stage and screen across the world as a sentimental message of healing and hope. With deliberate provocation, Ozick says it would have been better if the diary had been burned.

Ian Buruma opens up the argument in a brilliant article in the *New York Review of Books* (2/19/98). He says: "Anne Frank's diary, sold as a message of universal redemption, was actually something much better than that. For she was too intelligent to have written a simple message, redemptive or otherwise. What lifts this diary above the level of a mere witness account is the author's capacity to grapple with problems to which there are no easy answers. These include the problems of sexuality, growing up, and relations between parents and children, but also of being Jewish, of national belonging, religious faith, fate and personal freedom, the meaning of life, and of being denied the right to live. Since it contains so much, readers get different things from the diary, just as they would from any complex work."

No generic message of redemption

The point is that telling the truth about the Holocaust offers no slick comfort. Unlike the recent Holocaust movie

Life Is Beautiful, the Holocaust does not have a happy ending. There is no healing in this tragedy. Scholar Lawrence
Langer says in *Art from the Ashes: A Holocaust Anthology*
(1995) that in Holocaust literature we have to give up "the
comforting notion that suffering has meaning."

Another common lie is to show everything before the
Holocaust as idyllic. Before the Nazis came, and after they
left, life was beautiful. In contrast, Anita Lobel's grip-
pingly honest account of her survival in hiding and in a
Nazi concentration camp, *No Pretty Pictures: A Child of
War* (1998), reveals her strength and determination, but
also a far-from-perfect family before and after. Looking
back, she avoids sermonizing and analysis. She always felt
distant from her cold parents; it's the loss of Niania, the
nanny who raised and nurtured her, a woman who was
often anti-Semitic, that still breaks Lobel's heart.

But we don't want sensational accounts either, with
gruesome details of torment. As Holocaust survivor Ida
Fink said of her spare story collection, *A Scrap of Time
and Other Stories:* "I thought one should talk about these
things in a quiet voice" (*New York Times Book Review,*
7/12/87).

Personal accounts

It's the personal accounts that are the most powerful.

Art Spiegelman won a Pulitzer Prize for *Maus* (1986),
his autobiographical graphic novel in two volumes. It's
also available on CD-ROM. In grim cartoons, the Jews
are mice, the Poles are pigs, and the Nazis are cats, as
Spiegelman shows himself in New Jersey and in the

Catskills being told about the Holocaust by his Polish father, who survived Auschwitz. The candid account explores not only the concentration camp horror but also the guilt, love, and anger between father and son. Without a breath of sentimentality, this comic book talks about the monstrous truth of what happened in the camps and about what it is like to be the child of a survivor.

In *Nightfather* (1991), an autobiographical novel translated from the Dutch, another child of a Holocaust survivor, Carl Friedman, tells her story in a number of intense episodes about a young girl in the Netherlands in the 1950s and 1960s. She tells how her father's stories of his life in the camps are part of family life. Always, she and her brothers, Max and Simon, must listen to their father's stories of the camps. In one searing episode he describes the public hanging of his "Gypsy" (Romani) friend by the camp guards. Always, after his telling, there's a family argument: "If God exists," asks Max, "then why didn't he do something?"

Another autobiographical novel, Lutz Van Dijk's *Damned Strong Love: The True Story of Willi G. and Stefan K.* (1995), is one of the first books to dramatize the Nazi persecution of gays. It's based on the life of a Polish teenager whose love for an Austrian Nazi soldier led to capture, torture, and prison.

Elie Wiesel's *Night* (1960) is a stark personal memoir that takes up where Anne Frank left off. He describes what it was like for him as a young boy on the transports and in the camps, where his family died. In Auschwitz he watched his father break down and die. Then the boy was sent on to Buchenwald, where he was near starvation when the allies liberated the camps at the end of the war. His writing is plain. The facts are devastating. There is no redemption.

In his 1993 speech at the dedication ceremony of the U.S. Holocaust Memorial Museum in Washington, D.C., Wiesel made connections: "Anti-Semitism is the beginning, not the end of a disease. Prejudice knows no boundaries. When children are killed in Bosnia, it is our humanity that has failed.... We cannot tolerate the excruciating sights of this old new war."

Rescuers

Of course, many memoirs show that there were those who retained their humanity, who sacrificed for others, even in the darkest times. Most certainly, as Primo Levi says, though luck was the most important factor in survival, so also was the preservation of a moral sense, a refusal to see yourself and others as less than human. Lorenzo Perrone, an Italian civilian worker, saves Levi's life, first with food, but also because he helps Levi hold on to the belief that people can be good and therefore it is worth trying to live on. He sees Levi as a person. Levi, in the inferno, confronts the worst and the best in all of us.

One of the most inspiring rescuer stories is of Chiune Sugihara, the Japanese consul in Lithuania, who saved the lives of hundreds of Polish Jews by going against his government's orders and writing out visas that enabled the Jews to escape.

On a personal note, my husband, Hymie, was not a bystander. As a teenager in Cape Town in the 1950s he took part in the Defiance Campaign of resistance against apartheid, and he was arrested for sitting on a bench marked for "Non-Whites." And in the early 1960s, Hymie and I hid Nelson Mandela in our house when he was on the run. Mandela mentions it in his autobiography: "I stayed at a doctor's house in Johannesburg, sleeping in the servants' quarters at night, and working in the doctor's study during the day. Whenever anyone came to the house during the day, I would dash out to the backyard and pretend to be the gardener." From our house he went to hide for a much longer period with my cousin, also a Hazel, and her husband, Arthur Goldreich—and that place has now been turned into a museum.

But there is no happy ending. The questions of guilt and responsibility remain.

A Human Being Died That Night: A South African Story of Forgiveness (2003) by Pumla Gobodo-Madikizela is a searing account by a psychologist who grew up in South Africa's black townships and who served under Archbishop Tutu on the Truth and Reconciliation Commission (TRC). She brings you close to the horrific testimony about what apartheid's perpetrators did, and also to what Tutu called "holy" scenes of forgiveness by victims' families. But at the center are her personal prison interviews with Eugene de Kock, who directed "the blood, the bodies and the killing" against apartheid's enemies. Does he feel remorse? Can she feel empathy for him? Demonizing him as a monster, as hopelessly other, lets him—and us— off too easily, she maintains. She raises elemental issues about perpetrators, victims, and bystanders that stretch back to the Holocaust. How can apartheid President De Klerk say his hands were clean? What about the majority of whites who say they didn't know?

Michael Berenbaum, formerly of the U.S. Holocaust Memorial Museum and now president of the Survivors of the Shoah Visual History Foundation, speaks eloquently in his foreword to the Blackbirch Holocaust series about how the Holocaust raises moral questions in our lives right now:

> What prejudices do I have? . . . Am I certain—truly cer-
> tain—that I could not be a killer? That I would not sub-
> mit to the pressures of conformity and participate in
> horrible deeds, or, worse yet, embrace a belief that
> makes me certain—absolutely certain—that I am right
> and the others are wrong? That my cause is just and the
> other is an enemy who threatens me, who must be elim-
> inated?

These elemental questions bring me back to where I started. What about the bystander who doesn't kill, who just gets on with daily life and does nothing? Always there's the question: What would I have done?

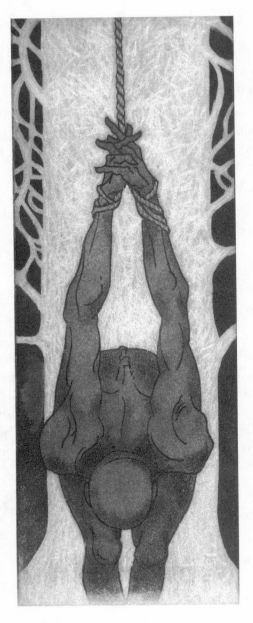

Blood Knot   TOM FEELINGS

The Silk Ball

TERRY DAVIS

CENTRAL LAOS—SUNRISE (1972)

High mountains, rugged and jumbled like the backs of a clan of aged dragons war-crazed from their battles in China. High and rugged and jumbled and green. Nappy green, green forested, grass green. And brown. Brown where bombs have scoured the green, where chemical defoliants have poisoned the green.

Soldiers walk a narrow mountain trail. All but two are Hmong. An American of mixed race walks in the middle of the line, and a Caucasian near the end. They are so much taller that the effect would be comic if the Hmong soldiers had a bounce to their walk—like Snow White and her company of Disney dwarfs hi-ho-ing home from work. But the weight of their weapons, the fatigue that dampens their steps, and the distant look in every set of eyes militate against humor. And so does their youth: They look like they should be in school uniforms, not combat fatigues.

The light-skinned black man, the shorter of the Americans, carrying the fewest weapons and the greatest number of shoulder bags, is Corporal WAYLAND LOVELACE, 19, of Edmond, Oklahoma, a navy corpsman in the employ of the CIA. Lovelace is as tired as anyone on the trail, but his heart shines bright with a pyrotechnic amalgam of belief and hope. Cpl. Lovelace has found himself here in the mountains of Laos, not as the warrior he sought to become in his days as a football player and two-time state champion wrestler for Edmond High, nor as the Navy SEAL he was competing to become until the CIA got wind of his test scores and his performance in physical training, plucked him out of his jump school graduation ceremony, and said they'd train him to be anything he wanted as long as he practiced the skill in secret in the mountains of Laos.

The ways in which Lovelace can kill you are legion: He will, in fact, rip your throat out with his teeth; he will drill one of your kidneys with a sharp stick until the breath from your mouth and nose cools in the palm of his other hand; he will pop a hole in your brain-housing group with his Swedish K, if circumstances call. But what thrills Cpl. Lovelace, and what he wants to do with all the days and nights of his life, not just back in the world but right here in these mountain forests and highland jungles, is to save you. It was as though the corpsman's training awakened something in Lovelace that he hadn't known was there, and the corpsman's life has moved the earth one planet closer to the sun, and the burst of illumination has transformed him. He will attend the University of Oklahoma, but not on the wrestling scholarship they offered him. Uncle Sugar will foot the bill for his four years, and another four of medical school. Lovelace will be a physician and a naval officer.

Cpl. Lovelace dreams these solar dreams and practices these mortal skills.

So young. And yet at 19, Cpl. Lovelace is two years older than the oldest of his Hmong brothers in arms.

Not all the Hmong are *brothers* in arms, however. The soldier at the head of the line is a sister.

PA KOU MOUA, 17, smokes an unfiltered Pall Mall. Her eyes are hard, her face worn as thoroughly as her GI fatigues, and yet her brown skin is lustrous through the dirt. She is a two-year veteran of the CIA's secret war in Laos.

Pa is not happy about this respite from combat. She knows that the more Communists she kills, the more deeply she endears herself to America. Captain Shepard has said this is so, and she believes Capt. Shepard. Nothing he has told her people has proven false. Everything they receive is number one: weapon, ration, supply, air support—all number one. Number one corpsman for

Hmong soldier and all Hmong people. United States number one.

Pa is not only courageous; she is insightful. She doesn't need Shepard telling her that there are plenty of Communists for her to kill. She knows, in fact, that there are too many Communists—in North Vietnam, South Vietnam, Laos, China—even for America to kill. And they are evil, like the Dab spirits, and like the Dab spirits, they hate the Hmong who live alone and free on the mountaintops. Unlike the Dab spirits, however, the Communists are not invisible, and when Pa Kou sees them, she grease them, she waste them, she rock and roll.

Pa has known for the past year, since the time of the big bomb, that America must lose the war. The company was positioned along a ridge in the mountains east of Sam Thong and the Nam Ngum River. NVA troops had been massing in the valley for an assault on the huge CIA base at Long Cheng to the south. Capt. Shepard said that a single bomb would be dropped, then they would reconnoitre. *A single bomb*, thought Pa. Shepard hunkered down between Pa and Cpl. Lovelace. He told Pa in Hmong that this would be the most powerful nonpoison bomb ever exploded. What he meant—and what he told Lovelace—was that it was non-nuclear. Pa had opened her mouth to ask about the poison bombs, but at that moment the breath was sucked from her lungs. A roar greater than the sum of all the thunder Pa had heard in her life cracked the earth and sky, the granite under their knees and fingertips kicked sharp and hard like the recoil of her .45 Colt, and viscous yellow flame boiled in the valley and rose up the mountain walls as though the sun had melted and yearned to climb back to its place in heaven and coalesce again.

That evening they reconnoitred the valley, but there was only desolation to observe. Nothing larger than an M-16 magazine remained of the thousands of NVA troops reported. Pa saw charred flakes of uniform, chunks of black bone, thready patches of the sun helmets the North Vietnamese regulars wear, metal that must have been artillery melted to the size and shape of elephant dung. There were no trees; no vegetation of any kind remained. But the thing that Pa could not hold in her mind was that the hills and streams that had textured the valley were gone. The streams were burnt dry and the hills were leveled. A single bomb had flattened the earth like the bottom of an old, dirty cook pan. There was no smell of burnt flesh as there always is after an air strike. A chemical smell clotted the air; it was like napalm, but Pa had seen no napalm drops produce such a landscape as this. *This must be what hell looks like—without the sinners,* Wayland had said. *Or maybe we're the sinners.* Capt. Shepard translated. *He says it looks like "Hell," the home of Ndu Nyong.*

Yes, Pa had thought, *the home of the Savage One at the top of the world where he imprisons Hmong souls in his great teak corral, devouring them in an eternal hunger.* "Hell," she thought. *So that is "Hell."*

A week later, over the mountains along the river west of Ban Na, they tracked two fresh NVA divisions. The Communists were moving south to prepare once more for a siege of Long Cheng. The Communists had reconnoitred the valley, too; they had seen the totality of destruction. And yet they had not turned around and marched home. It was clear to Pa that the Communists were crazy, and that all the might of America would not stop them.

America would not save Vietnam or Laos. America would not save the Hmong. But America took care of her friends, Capt. Shepard said, and nobody was a better friend to America than a soldier like Pa Kou who fought alongside a United States Marine. *If I could, Pa,* Shepard had said, *I'd make you a certified jarhead myself. You practice your English.*

And so Pa practiced her English, and hoped in her secret heart that when the retreat came they would take her with them back to America. Her secret heart beat a prideful cadence to the words Shepard had taught her.

PA KOU (VOICE-OVER)

> Born in woods,
> Raised by bear,
> Double set dog teeth,
> Triple coat hair.
> Two brass ball,
> Cast-iron rod.
> I mean motherfucker.
> I Marine, by God!

CHENG MOUA, 16, Pa's brother, struggles to hide his joy at their break from combat. Unlike his sister and the rest of the Hmong, who hate the Communists with all their warrior hearts, Cheng is on the CIA payroll because it's the best pay around. Cheng's heart would like to follow the shaman's path, but a shaman is paid in chickens and pigs. And Cheng has never known a shaman with such fine, sturdy footwear as his GI boots.

At this moment Cheng's heart is pumping hard up the rocky path of longing. In addition to his joy, he struggles to hide his tumescence in contemplation of the young women who will play the ball game tonight, and the possibilities after the ball game. He imagines his hand around the silk ball, its smooth surface on his fingertips, its heft in his palm.

The taller white man, Captain STEVE SHEPARD, 32, is a ten-year veteran CIA advisor to counterinsurgency forces. He wears a soft, wide-brimmed floppy hat, a fatigue blouse with the sleeves cut off, a flak vest, fatigue pants. His skin is tanned as dark as that of his Hmong brothers in arms. He is six feet, four inches tall and weighs 180 pounds. He carries an AK-47 slung on one shoulder and a .45 in a shoulder holster under the other. He wears a webbed belt from which magazines for the AK and the Colt dangle like rectangular charms on an olive-drab charm bracelet. High on his chest, opposite the .45, a Gerber fighting knife hangs handle down in its scabbard from a strap of his haversack. In 1962 the CIA recruited Marine First Lieutenant Shepard out of the Military

Language Institute in Monterey, California, where he learned Lao, Hmong, and the major Montagnard dialects.

Shepard has a bad feeling. It's as though he's the only white grain of sand left among the darker grains in an hourglass the size of Southeast Asia. He is not the only white one, but he and Cpl. Wayland Lovelace, his Afro-Okie super corpsman with the high and lonesome name, are among the few remaining. He feels a pull more powerful and complex than gravity. He hears the distant roar of a thousand thousand souls as they accelerate downward into a teeming darkness. American support for the war could end any day, which is why, for the first time in his three tours, Shepard is pulling his troops out of the field so they can attend their New Year Festival.

These Hmong people have been at war with some greater power since before Genghis Khan subjugated China and laid waste to Asia Minor, since before Christ fulfilled his destiny on the cross. So why sit out their New Year Festival on account of a little danger, a little peril, a little foreboding, a little doom? Why ruin the biggest holiday of the year and a chance for these young men to meet a girl and make a wife?

Maybe there is a gift in the Hmong's doomed alliance with America: Because so many of them have died, there are plenty of prospective brides to choose from. Let them ditch their fighting clothes and put on the holiday duds their mothers have kept folded and wrapped in a prayer.

As long as they make sure their sidearm is handy and their M-16 not far away.

And what of Shepard's girl soldier, Moua Pa Kou, his junior jarhead, as smart and fearless a little badger as he has ever seen? What will Pa Kou ever do back in the world where women taking scalps is a figure of speech? It doesn't matter what Pa will do; she deserves a chance, and she will have no chance here. Shepard has vowed two things: One, not to allow Pa to be taken alive; and two—if they actually do swim out of this shit—to get her back to the States even if he has to adopt her.

The truth is that, although Shepard has never fathered a child, he already thinks of Pa as a daughter, and worse, he has come to think of Lovelace as a son. They are so, so young—their lethal skills notwithstanding. These are not the sentiments about his troops that a wise commander carries into battle. But there it is. The ball is unraveling, and it's rolling way too fast now for anyone to catch.

The Communist forces would like few things better than to wipe out these Hmong—these *Meo,* these mountain barbarians—who have been a constant rain of sharp stones on their heads for too many years, who will have, when all this is over, set back the Communist victory by ten years.

The Communists are not happy with Captain Shepard, either, and they have posted a bounty for his head.

HMONG VILLAGE—MORNING

This is the *ban*, the village, where four Hmong clans will meet for feasting, reunion with relatives, placation of the spirits through animal sacrifice, fun—including fornication for those of courting age—and more feasting in celebration of the New Year.

The smoke of cooking fires rises from each *jah*, from each house. It's chilly on this December morning, not that a fire provides much warmth when the wind blows through the openings in the plank walls. This is because the planks aren't milled; they are split from the log with an axe and wedge. No windows in the *jah*s. When you want to see outside, you look through the wall. Every *jah* is constructed so that one of the doors allows a view of the mountain across the way. These people need to remind themselves that they can pick up stakes and hike over to that other mountain and start a new life anytime they feel like it. They also need to move their villages often because the mountain soil is easily depleted, and because the animal waste builds up to intolerable levels before the monsoons wash it away.

Yes, it's a primitive life. No running water, no plumbing, dirt floor, shelter for livestock built onto the house. There's no smell from the animal waste today, though, and there won't be for a while because the monsoons of November washed the horseshit, cowshit, pigshit, chickenshit down the mountain. The Hmong design their buildings so that this takes place. Make no mistake:

Primitive is not a synonym for *stupid*. Nor does the word suggest a lack of personal hygiene. Actually, they do have running water. They just don't have it in the house. Their water is a clear-running stream.

This is an agrarian society, a preindustrial, preliterate society. Before the CIA armed them they were hunting game with crossbows and the occasional flintlock. Before AID, the Agency for International Development, came to Southeast Asia, they were plowing their fields with sharp sticks. They grow corn to feed themselves and their livestock; they grow rice. They also grow opium for cash.

The population of one hundred has doubled today because of the festival. The wide paths between houses are clogged with smiling, waving Hmong.

At the edge of the village, a wooden structure with a steeply pitched roof and open front and sides runs twenty meters along the mountainside. It looks like a picnic shelter in the city park of a little town in the States. It is, in fact, a shelter for the market where every Monday people from the smaller villages come to buy and sell meat, vegetables, cotton cloth and cotton filler for quilts and quilted clothing, soap, tools, radios, cassette recorders and tapes, flashlights and batteries, canned tuna from Taiwan, opium, a variety of candy taken in trade from American GIs for opium, Coleman lanterns procured in the same fashion, and the most sought-after item of all: tampons.

MARKET SHELTER—DAY

Festivities take place in homes all over the village, but
most people are here. For two reasons: One, the region's
most powerful shaman is about to cut up a pig and
entreat various spirits with its internal organs before hanging it on the spit to placate people's appetites; some folks,
particularly the aged, are here to take part in this invoca-
tion. Two, every young person is here because every other
young person is here, so this is where they'll get maxi-
mum exposure. Kids of courting age—fifteen, sixteen,
seventeen years old—smolder through the morning in
anticipation of evening when they will play the ball game.
The young women are demure, the young men distracted. The preadolescent boys, who will not play the
ball game today, are goofy. The preadolescent girls, who
will not play the ball game today but who dream of the
silk ball slipping through their hands and with its fall the
handing over of an article of clothing to the handsome
boy, the clever boy, the graceful boy who tossed the ball,
are giddy on this day of exquisite sensual delight. This day
of heightened vascular response.

Cpl. Lovelace, with Pa Kou attempting to translate,
makes rounds of the sick among the villagers. He is
allowed to lance a boil on the buttocks of a woman who
has been unable to sit or to lie on her back for days. He
powders the boil with sulfa and applies a field dressing.
He is asked to cure an ailing goat, which he is happy to
try. But the goat won't tell him where it hurts, and Pa
does not speak goat. The two young warriors laugh, and

the goat's owner laughs along. A shaman gets most of the doctor work around here.

But the shaman has a ritual function today. His bell, rattle, and drum resound in the thin mountain air among the voices of birds as distinct and resonant as the report of an M-16 or an AK. They are kindred sounds in that both tear the cloth of life to allow the issue of another wave of spirits. There is the instant ripped squeal of the pig when the shaman draws his knife through its throat and frees the shining, syrupy blood, and with it thanks the Neng spirits, the helping spirits, for their devotion to the Hmong in their daily battle against the Dab, the legion of invisible demons, stealth troops, who search and destroy in service of Ndu Nyong, the Savage One. The Dab are eternal, numberless as stars, and possessed of vindictive memories as searing and adhesive as napalm.

ON A GRASSY FIELD,

cozied up against the mountain in the shade of two giant pines, children in festival costume sit in a rough circle before Cheng Moua. Cheng is shed of his combat clothes and dressed in a plain black shirt and pants. The music and voices and the fragrance of roasting pig are faint here, swept down the mountain by the breeze through the pine boughs.

Cheng sits with his back against the thicker of the pines. It is Cheng's role today, and his pleasure, to tell the children a story. This is a storytelling culture. It was, in fact, until the twentieth century, a culture without a written language.

Capt. Shepard, laden with shoulder bags and a spool of wire the size of a basketball, walks across the field toward the trees and the defense perimeter at the edge of the steep downslope. He waves the spool and wishes Cheng and the children good fortune in the new year. They wave back, the children amazed that this white man speaks their language. Shepard smiles at the radiant faces of the kids, and at the thought of Moua Cheng, Pa Kou's brother, in a function he can perform capably. When Shepard has disappeared through the pines, Cheng begins.

CHENG

Once upon a time in the morning of creation,
thousands of years before the fall of the Hmong
Kingdom and our dispersal south, a multitude of
spirits shared the world with us. One such race
of spirits was the Dab. They walked among us in
their lazy way, trusting, and absent of the will to
harm any creature—animal, human, or fellow spirit.

Cheng looks toward the market shelter and tilts his head. He looks back at the children.

CHENG

Today, at the beginning of the new year, our shaman
entreats the Neng spirits to protect us from the Dab,
whose only joy is dealing the People pain and death.

What power intervened to twist their placid hearts to
hate and ignite their torpid natures to a practice of the
most ambitious cruelty? Was it Ndu Nyong who pierced
them with a fetid claw?

No, it was not the Savage One. We were that power.
We brought upon ourselves the Dab's eternal enmity.
We the People.

The faces of the boys and girls are rapt. Feasting is forgotten, their fine clothes, play, presents, all forgotten.

CHENG

The Dab are invisible now, but once upon a time,
in the dawning of the world, they were the most
visible of spirits, and we saw that they have no
skin. The Dab were an unsettling stew of organ,
bone, and thin strands of muscle, their hearts
pump-pumping in their narrow chests,
their blood coursing like strings of fireflies
against a dusty sunset. It was their peaceful,
trusting equanimity that kept them whole.

THE STORY WORLD

is the Hmong Eden, a peaceable kingdom where cobra
and mongoose twirl and play, and the smiling Hmong
share village and forest paths with the sexless, transparent
Dab who smile in return with shy raised eyes before they
look away again.

CHENG (V.O.)

The Dab existed in the shape of the People, and
the People knew that we ourselves possessed a
similar intricately layered and vital interior. But
the Dab were graphic, and the Dab were foreign.
And the Dab were the most vulnerable creatures
ever to walk the earth.

Over time a voice rose in the hearts of the People,
and this voice whispered, *The Dab are not of the
People. The Dab are other*. And over time the
voice whispered louder, *The Dab are weak, and
the People are strong*.

The People's smiles became superior, and then
aggressive. The wonder with which we gazed at
the inner workings of a Dab life turned to contempt.
The Dab stopped meeting our eyes. They trundled
off the trail when the People approached.

A man whose superiority smolders in his eyes walks the
path to the village pool. Dab fall away before him, seared
by his contempt. A Dab standing at the pool edge, lost in
the beauty of morning sun filtered through pines into
pristine water, does not see this man reach out his arm.

CHENG

It was a day that changed the world when one of
the People thrust his hand between the ribs of a Dab
who had not observed his approach. The Dab
turned. His eyes flared black with bewilderment and
then with fear. The man's skin-armored fingers

clenched the Dab heart, ripped it from the Dab chest
like a beet from the earth, and waved it high
in a banner of blood. In these moments the Dab
became a fountain, a gory monument to the cruel
threads in the human cloth. Blue-tinged blood
leaped from the Dab's ragged veins and bright
red blood from his surging arteries.

The man in whose hand the Dab heart pumped slower
and slower felt his strength expand as the bloody
thing deflated. When the heart lay empty and still,
and the Dab had fled, crying to his fellow spirits his
pain and bewilderment, the man felt as he had never
felt before. A new power had entered the world,
and he proclaimed to all this power of the strong
over the weak.

Madness grips the People. They visit limitless cruelties
upon the Dab.

CHENG (V.O.)

Soon the People were plucking organs from the Dab
like thick, wet, waxy fruit.

The Dab congregate to make their exodus. They look like
clear-plastic sacks of life burst open and spilling.

CHENG (V.O.)

We saw the Dab as fully visible beings for the
final time during their exodus into the mountains
at the edge of the world. With each step in their

flight the Dabs' fear turned to hatred, and with
this hatred grew a transparent skin that held them
together in the absence of their better nature.

The Dab climb through forest into a landscape of gray
sand, gray rock, slate-blue sky, higher and higher where
the wind howls with the constant and eternal desolation
of lost souls.

CHENG (V.O.)

When they reached the domain of Ndu Nyong, the
Dab's hatred had transformed them. There, in his
vast corral, where the rock surface is always freshly
puddled with the blood of Hmong he devours, where
beyond the towering teak corral fence the world
stops and the rushing black of nothingness begins,
the Dab pledged to the Savage One their eternal
allegiance in exchange for a shroud of invisibility
in which to practice forever their revenge upon
the People.

UNDER THE PINES

the story is over. The boys and girls are quiet. The boys
look at one another; the girls only raise their eyes.

One boy makes claws of his fingers and goes for a ticklish
spot on the girl next to him. He reaches in and extracts a
vital part. She screams. He waves the imaginary organ in
the air.

BOY

I got something! I hope it's not her pooper!

The boys go after the girls, pull out imaginary organs, and proclaim them. The girls scream.

Cheng smiles. He's glad these kids have a few years yet to disbelieve, or not to care.

BACK AT THE MARKET SHELTER,

the flowing blood is not Hmong, nor is it Dab. It is pig blood, sacrificial, brought forth in entreaty, in hope, and in faith that it will lessen the flow of Hmong blood in the world, lighten the load of pain, and enlist the help of sympathetic spirits against the invisible, vengeful Dab.

Among this day's delights to the senses add the constant subtle timpani of the silver coins attached by silver chains that adorn the female costumes. The coins clink when the girls and women walk, and bounce forth a soft silver chant when the girls run and the coins lift off the surface of their hats and blouses.

Pa Kou, Cpl. Lovelace, and other soldiers chow down on pig. Pa Kou will not play the ball game today, because in her secret warrior's heart Pa Kou is already betrothed. Cpl. Lovelace is focused on Pa as though she were an elegantly crafted explosive device with six seconds on the timer. He yearns to be extinguished in her blast.

IN THE FOREST

North Vietnamese Army soldiers—astonishingly youth-ful—younger even than the Hmong soldiers, each with an AK-47 slung on his shoulder, walk single file along a forest trail.

AND PULL BACK TO REVEAL that they are members of an NVA squad.

AND FARTHER BACK TO REVEAL that the squad is leading an NVA company up the mountain.

AND FARTHER BACK TO REVEAL that the company is part of an NVA force that keeps coming and coming and never ends.

But what are those red, wispy flashes among the troops? They appear in the air, then disappear, moving forward at the soldiers' pace. The size of apples, grapefruits, egg-plants, they pulse, go dim, fade out, pulse again. Faint body-shapes coalesce around them, then fade. It is as though there are barely visible naked beings among the NVA. The Dab have come to join the attack. They glow with the pleasure they anticipate.

AT THE MARKET SHELTER

women and adolescent girls clean up the aftermath of the feast. Men take down the tables and move the plywood and sawhorses. The adolescent girls' eyes seek the older girls clustered like quail in the shade of the hillside. Now the young girls' eyes shift to the rousing advance of the boys who toss the bright balls of silk into the air.

The boys' faces are full of hope as they trace the rising, whirling patches of color, then follow the soft descent into their waiting palms.

An engine rumbles to life, then idles back. Colored lights blink on all around the shelter's roof line. A Caterpillar industrial generator sits like a squatty yellow rhino at the side of the building. The familiar yellow paint and the name in black look odd so far from home. The CIA has a long reach, and—at least in the first half of this decade— limitless money. Behind the generator, stacked against the hill, rises a bank of fifty-gallon drums of gasoline.

ON THE GRASSY FIELD—DUSK

A man stands on a boulder embedded in the mountain-side. He is blowing into something that looks like a bamboo machine gun. It's a *khene*, a giant flute, and it makes a sound like a long-legged bird caught in a snare and resigned to its death.

Sunset bursts from the western horizon like neon lava, a fountain of gold sizzling toward the zenith of the sky, a wave of red, pink, then purple at the edges, flowing east-ward, turning black, encasing these mountains in the shell of night.

AT THE MARKET SHELTER

Finally, the ball game: the parallel arcs of three dozen silk balls, the sleek streaming tracings of tradition spinning before the eyes of these Hmong clans the union of man and woman.

Cheng Moua is here, wearing a black hat now, and a red sash, along with other soldiers in more elaborate festival costume. They stand outside the shelter in the mist of colored light showering down from the roof. They throw like slow-pitch softball pitchers, arcing the ball up through the rainbow mist into the purple-gray dusk.

Cheng's ball is yellow with red and gold. It arcs downward from the dusky sky back into the colored light, spinning like a tiny, ringed planet. His partner, BEE, 15, bats it out of the air and sends it rolling across the grass, through the legs of a boy five boys down. When Cheng returns to his place he sees Bee's hat on the grass at her feet.

That's how it works: you drop the ball, you lose an article of clothing.

Cheng looks up at Bee's coy smile; then he lofts the ball again. This time she makes the catch. She winds up and flings the ball two meters over Cheng's head.

CHENG

A throw that bad counts as a miss!

BEE

Those rules are from the other side of the mountain!

Silk balls arc in splendor through the cool evening air, are caught and dropped, dropped and caught. Piles of clothing rise.

Mothers smile at the vision of grandchildren who will issue from unions born this night, imagine holding those sweet babies to their shoulders, imagine the baby fragrance of that baby hair, the nibbly taste of those baby ears.

Fathers frown at the young women dropping, dropping the balls thrown by their sons, frown at the thought of the staggering bride prices that the fathers of these beautiful girls will demand.

Shepard observes these moments of *La Comédie Humaine.* He knows this could be anywhere in the world, these Hmong people any people. He is too fatigued and too encumbered with knowledge to do anything but shake his head.

IN A *JAH,*

in a dark corner, overspread with light from a kerosene lantern so silent and gold and thick and translucent that it blankets them like pollen, Pa Kou Moua and Wayland Lovelace make love.

Pa is on top, not supporting herself on her knees, but rather squatting, the quadricep muscles leaping in the sweat-greased golden shadows of her thighs. When she rises she nearly separates from Wayland, but she slows as she reaches her apex; she crimps and shudders in her commitment not to leave him behind. In this moment light flows between them. Golden light. And Pa is the sky, and Wayland the earth. And a golden ribbon of sunset is the horizon between, with the dark isthmus of Lovelace connecting them. And then Pa descends, consuming Wayland again in the warm Pa sea, so deep, as deep as all the straining height of him. And when this moment ends, Pa is on the rise again.

Pa's eyes are closed, but Wayland is watching. He will not miss one beat of this feast of the senses. Wayland does, in fact, simultaneously see, feel, smell, hear, and taste their lovemaking. What he hears, along with their breathing, is the whisper of sea-tide rising into an estuary that will never hold the flood. What he tastes is the sea—and blood, and sweat, because much work is required to batter down ecstasy's walls, particularly when the combat itself so sustains us that we almost hate to see the walls fall; and as they begin to topple we may not wish to enter, we may hold back our breath; but when the implosion finally comes, the vacuum sucks us out of our battle gear and our skin and our senses into the round, warm, rocking sea of memory where above us a heart beats in place of the sun. And Wayland smells the Pa Kou sea, rising over him, pulling him to the dark, warm center of himself where she has taken him over and over but cannot take him often enough.

Pa rests on her knees now, nothing between them except the isthmus of Wayland Lovelace projecting into the Pa sea. They are one pulsing shadow. Not even Pa Kou Moua, known by all to be strong and mean as a badger after walking these mountains, killing VC and Pathet Lao and NVA, has the power in her quads to dance this step all night. She has led them to the ramparts, and she now takes them up the ladder with . . . *with wand'ring steps and slow*, as Eve led Adam out of the lobotomized tranquility of Eden into the travail of the human world where knowledge is the price we pay to seek the chalice of joy, where the only paths are pain, the only destination death.

IN THE FOREST

the vast NVA force moves through the trees.

An NVA heavy mortar company deploys at the base of the mountain.

NVA soldiers rise up the mountain toward the village like a flood, encompassing, awesome in power, and detached as an act of nature.

IN THE VILLAGE

Pa, Lovelace, and other soldiers, some still in festival clothes, walk from the shadows between the *jah*s. Shepard walks behind.

A dark weight has settled in Shepard's eyes. His dread has deepened. He is about to dig in on a mountaintop where high hopes and great expectations run rampant. Perfect conditions for a tornado of pain. Shepard knows that fate loves irony. This is among the laws of the universe. Tonight the village is an invitation to mayhem. He has allowed a third of his force to go courting, and he has his corpsman manning a bunker on his defense perimeter. This is why Shepard spent the afternoon setting mines and trip flares across a three-hundred-meter span of hillside.

Each soldier settles into a sandbagged bunker twenty meters apart where the downslope begins.

Night falls like smoke. A breath ago the trees were green; now they are black.

AT THE MARKET SHELTER—NIGHT

has fallen. The colored lights are feeble against the immensity of this mountain-forest dark. Everyone drops the ball now, every girl, every boy. They see it only when it's about to bounce off their noses.

All along the line boys shed a shirt, a shoe, a sock onto the pile of clothing in front of them. But now when a girl misses she stops as though the game were over. And soon, all the girls have stopped. And so now the game is over. The girls have disrobed to the point where modesty demands that the next round of this ritual take place in private.

The girls turn to one another with looks that say, *Goodbye, friends of my youth.* And they walk off toward home, leaving behind on the ground the beautiful costumes sewn in anticipation of moments soon to come. *Goodbye! Good luck!*

Cheng and all the boys dress in haste. But when they bend to gather the clothing of the departed girls, they fold and stack the garments with care.

The boys go their various ways, carrying with reverence, with hope, with erotic longing, and with a measure of fear this redolent bundle. They will take off their festival costumes, put on casual clothes in which—if their longings are fulfilled—to lie on the forest loam, and then they will walk quietly to their partner's *jah*, return the garments she lost in the ball game, and invite her out for a night of love. If the love goes well, the two will ask their parents to arrange a marriage.

ON THE DEFENSE PERIMETER

Lovelace . . . , Pa . . . , Shepard . . . peer out into the dark from behind their sandbags along the top of the steep, forested hillside. They shift when they hear noises in the trees behind them. They know this is a lovers' night and that the woods to the rear will be filled with whispers and stirrings. But the sounds float up, sift through the trees, carry out over the perimeter, and hang in the air like their own longings and fears given earthly substance.

AT THE *JAH* OF BEE'S FAMILY

Cheng raps on the wall. He whispers into the golden light pouring through the cracks between the planks.

Someone moves inside, and the golden streams of light cease, then flow again as a body passes between the kerosene lamp and the wall. Then around the corner glides Bee, dark and lovely. She wears soft black pants and a soft black blouse. Her black hair glistens.

Cheng extends the armload of clothing resting on his upturned helmet. Bee bends to set it on the ground and bangs her head on the stock of his M-16. She gives Cheng a comic scowl and rubs her head.

Cheng and Bee follow the beam of Cheng's flashlight into the darkness.

ON THE HILLSIDE

NVA soldiers lie on their bellies, fingertip to fingertip, in a line across the hillside. Each man sweeps his arms with mortal care over the ground within his arms' reach, walking his fingertips like night spiders through pine needles, twigs, moss, rocks, and around trees, feeling for trip wires, feeling for the fresh dirt that indicates a recently buried mine, yearning for the steel touch of the leg of a Claymore. When each man has searched every centimeter of the arm-length of ground in front of him, he extends his arms outward again and finds the fingertips of his comrades, and then the entire line of men hunches up the hill like a single living creature through the space its many arms have swept.

ON THE PERIMETER

Shepard..., Pa..., Lovelace... squint their eyes to penetrate the night.

ON THE OUTSKIRTS OF THE VILLAGE

entwined couples move with ecstatic, clumsy stealth through the woods. Some carry flashlights, some lanterns, others stumble in the dark.

Cheng and Bee come to an enormous fir tree, the boughs of which brush the ground. Cheng parts the boughs and follows as Bee crawls under, into the soft, scented, hidden chamber.

ON THE HILLSIDE

NVA fingers walk the forest floor in the grave-black dark. The back of a hand makes contact with a wire. The hand stops, a voice whispers, the hand signals. Everything stops. The NVA soldiers rise as a wave, flow over the wire and back again to union with the earth.

Fingers step into a drift of fresh dirt, moist, smelling of the farm, of home, and of hands that held American ciga-rettes...and stop, and brush at the dirt oh so lightly...un-til the dome of an M-25 antipersonnel mine is exposed. Hands place over the M-25 a white plastic two-gallon jug with the bottom cut out. A red haze pulses faintly, illumi-nating a label on the jug: Clorox Bleach. Where would Communist forces get Clorox? From the GIs' trash dumps.

Among the moving forms of soldiers the jugs appear a smoky gray, like the heads of ghosts rising from the earth.

Fingers navigate the forest loam through pine needles, over twigs, foliage, branches...until the fingertips touch metal. And the fingers stop...and wait...and take a slow, deep breath to summon a lover's patience...and then stretch and grasp one metal leg, and then another. Fingers hold the firing wire...as fingers lift and rotate the Claymore mine until, in the hazy red glow, the admonition imprinted on the body of the mine TOWARD ENEMY now points uphill.

ON THE PERIMETER

Shepard sees a faint, gauzy red glow, like vaguely luminescent apples, on the limbs of the pines and firs he cannot see. He thinks of the light of the Idaho State Police car that lured him and his brother out of bed one night through fog so thick they swam their arms to the country road where they saw their first dead body, a soldier, a boy they had watched star in three sports at Wallace High, draped like a spike buck over the hood of a '40 Merc coupe, one of his combat boots caught by a buckle in the driver's side windshield wiper.

But there's no fog tonight.

Shepard squints, and the points of red haze congeal; he widens his eyes and the red goes hazy again. He imagines the beating hearts of an invisible army.

ON THE HILLSIDE

a porcupine climbs down a pine tree and waddles through the crawling NVA.

A soldier sees the porky trundling toward him, and he sees the trip wire that he has avoided. With a pine branch the soldier lifts the wire . . . and the porky clears it by a quill.

The soldier breathes deep and sets down the branch with care. He stretches the arm that held the branch, then rests his elbow on the ground. The last sound he hears in the world is the click of an M-25 detonator.

AT CHENG AND BEE'S FIR TREE

urgent vocalizations echo in the dark. These are sounds, not words. The love warblings of young animals. Passionate, quizzical, resonant with wonder and release.

A blast of high explosives fractures this transcendent moment. Cheng hits his flashlight. The two scramble for their clothes in a rain of fir needles.

They emerge on hands and knees. Cheng gives Bee the flashlight. They give each other a look, the dominant emotion of which is fear, and go to their separate duties.

ON THE PERIMETER

the blast of the mine tears a fiery hole in the dark. Shepard, Pa, Lovelace, the rest of the soldiers look over their sandbags down the hill.

ON THE HILLSIDE

smoke rises and pine needles burn around the meter-wide crater left by the explosion. In the sparse, shifting light of the flames wounded NVA soldiers stifle their cries. One wounded soldier sees something that scares him worse than his injury.

The head and shoulder of the man killed by the mine

move along the ground, uphill. The stump of his arm compels his comrades to follow.

The wounded soldier scrambles away from this apparition . . . until he scrambles into a wire that trips a flare that splashes white sputtery phosphorescent light over thirty meters.

Among the things illuminated is the disembodied head and shoulder continuing up the hill. It moves because it is stuck to the quills of the porcupine.

ON THE PERIMETER

Shepard raises a fat-barreled flare gun high above his head and fires.

On the hillside below flares are tripped left and right. An M-25 goes off, then another, then another flare, and another mine, all along the three-hundred meter stretch of hillside.

Shepard's flare trails red sparks, ignites, floats back down on its tiny parachute, turning night to day.

But it is a surreal, phosphorescent daylight that reveals the mountain alive with enemy, some still crawling, some on their feet, charging up the mountain.

SHEPARD

Mother Christ.

He expected bad news, but he didn't expect it in battalion strength. He jumps on the radio and calls in air support.

He gives the coordinates of his own position and says they need to unload a little short.

Pa, Lovelace, all the village defenders fire down the hill. A .30 caliber machine gun opens up, its red tracers reaching down into the darkness like thin, sizzling wires. The *whump...whump...whump* of a light mortar joins the fusillade.

Shepard turns to his Claymore detonators, flips up the bale on each and brings down the side of his fist on the one, two, three, four, five, six handles.

ON THE HILLSIDE—PHOSPHORESCENT DAYLIGHT

In *real* time, elements in this sequence take place simultaneously. But this is a *surreal* world, and *surreal* time.

SLOW MOTION: The Claymore opens like a plastic
     flower with petals of fire and smoke, with a
          thunderous concussion so deep it fractures the
               world and shreds the pieces into plasma of earth
                    and air and rock and plant and human being.

Thirty meters down the hill steel balls propelled by the
     blast cut through a fir tree thicker than a man,
          cut it clean as the single blow of a nightmare axe.

Steel balls cut through standing NVA, vaporize the upper
     portions of these men in a cranberry mist, leave the
          lower portions standing as the upper portion of
               the fir tree topples down among them and
                    the blast blows everything away.

The Dab are glazed with this gory stew. They glisten for a beat like the first bright crackle of a blood-fluorescent tube. Their anticipation grows with the carnage.

Crawling NVA are seared by the heat of the blast and terrorized by the supersonic passage of instant death a half-meter above their heads. Their terror is such that they do not feel the drenching bath of blood and tissue.

SLOW MOTION: A Claymore sits on a pine branch like a clumsy plastic bird, then it melts, and, in a reanimation of fire and simultaneous volcanic dissonance both awful and awesome, it gives birth to seven-hundred tiny steel offspring.

The steel flock fans downward, fifty meters to the right, to the left, and a hundred meters down the hill. The steel birdlets make up in velocity and vehemence what they lack in grace of flight. They fly *through* all substances they encounter, except rock, thick wood, the earth itself.

Standing men are separated from themselves at the level of their hairlines, eyes, noses, lips, chins, necks, shoulders, nipples. . . .

Crawling men are drilled through like berries.

Inside the cacophony of explosion and supersonic slipstream are the hundreds of audible punctures of flesh and bone. Individual drops of steel rain. Minute decibels of death.

The balls fly through the Dab, between their organs,
glowing for a millisecond within the vacuum of
Dab spirit-flesh.

SLOW MOTION: A Claymore sits on the ground on
its metal legs. Taped to the front of the plastic body
of the mine is a Baggie full of yellow powder: It is
CS gas—tear gas. The mine bulges, cracks.
Flames grin at the prospect of emergence into
the world. The Baggie melts; the powder
bubbles, glows orange, matures
into vapor, merges with the air.

The heat of the fireball pushes a fan-shaped yellow cloud
through the shredded bodies, through the wounded,
out among the NVA who have not taken cover.
They gasp, cough, weep, drain mucus like a
hoard of supplicants possessed by the angel
of phlegm. They cannot see. But they
can feel the upsloping ground. And
they keep coming.

A Claymore sits on the ground on its metal legs. Unlike
the others, this one is pointed up the hill.

ON THE PERIMETER

Shepard, Pa, Lovelace watch over their sandbags the pro-
gressive Claymore explosions. ONE: Pa thinks of her
brother, Cheng. She hopes he has remembered his
weapon, his helmet, his flak vest. She hopes he finds her
bunker. She wishes that he had chosen the shaman's bell,

rattle, and drum. TWO: *Any other night,* Shepard is thinking. *Any other night, any other circumstance, I could have defended this mountain.* THREE: Lovelace stands and rips with his stubby Swedish K.

LOVELACE

Momma, this is the shit now. We are gettin' it now. Blue eighty-two! Blue eighty-two!

FLASHBACK—THE BIG BOMB

It reminds me of a play we ran in football, Lovelace told Capt. Shepard. They lay on the cool granite of the ridge and watched the bomb fall from the cargo doors of the C-130. A black dot, like a turd out of a rabbit. Even through the captain's binoculars it didn't look like a bomb, because it had no fins. It was a fat cylinder, rounded on one end and pointed on the other, strapped to a wooden pallet, floating down on a big cargo parachute. Big Blue, Shepard said they called it. BLU-82. The NVA in the valley didn't even fire at the plane. Shepard reached for the binoculars. *I was a wide receiver,* Lovelace said, *that was my play. Blue eighty-two.* He held out his hands as though a gently spiraling ball were about to nestle there and get toted for six.

The concussion was like God's hand clapping down over the valley. Lovelace thought the pressure would suck his eyeballs out. The mountain shook hard one time, like it had taken a punch, and he felt the rock heat up through his pants. The valley boiled in a thick soup of fire. Waves of flame unfurled against the mountain walls like the tongues of giant hungry things. It was terrible and beautiful. It was biblical, and God was on America's side. *Our team!* Lovelace yelled at Shepard through the roar. *It's our team did that!*

When they could stand again, Lovelace danced with his fists in the air as he had when he'd scored a touchdown, or pinned his man in a match. He and Pa high-fived, and banged their fists together. That night they made love for the first time.

BACK TO SCENE

                         LOVELACE
      Blue eigh—

SLOW MOTION: Superheated steel balls fly at Lovelace in a concentrated mass, like a darkly molten fist.

   The sandbags burst in a storm of earth and cotton flakes burnt black. And Cpl. Wayland Lovelace bursts, adding a watery red, forcing the dark storm toward purple.

Nothing is left of Lovelace's position: no sandbags, no Lovelace, no nothing.

SLOW MOTION: Steel balls veer from the mass, zero in on Pa like killer bees.
   Pa turns toward the dark cyclonic rush, screams. All the balls but one fly over her head. The low-trajectory ball pierces her cheek, traverses her

open mouth, exits through the other cheek.
The white-hot flash sears her exposed
flesh and the blast flings her backward
like a scrap of paper in a gale.

Shepard hustles to Pa. Her face is burnt black, her eyes open, the hole in her cheek cauterized. Her mouth moves. Shepard speaks to her in Hmong. From a pouch on his belt he pulls a syringe of morphine and jabs the needle into her neck. He looks at her face and sees how it is that her eyes are open: They are fused with the surrounding skin. He grabs for a second syringe and a third, and he does the most generous thing one human being can do for another: He puts Moua Pa Kou to sleep.

IN THE VALLEY

the NVA mortar company is set up. Every man looks up at the white glow rising on the hillside. A command is given. In each team a man drops a shell into a mortar tube and turns away.

ON THE PERIMETER

everything happens at once now: The last two Claymores blow; the first NVA heavy mortar rounds land in the village; fires roar; men, women, children scream pain, terror, the names of loved ones.

Soldiers who played the ball game, one of whom is Cheng, sprint out of the trees. His helmet bounces off his head. The M-16 seems huge in his hands—like a cartoon gun.

AK-47 fire rattles like popcorn. Rounds strike trees, sandbags, running men.

Shepard lobs a grenade in front of his position, then sprints for his bunker.

The grenade explodes ten meters downhill from where he dives for cover. Cries of wounded NVA rise as dirt, vegetation, flesh, and bone hail down.

Cheng hits the dirt in a storm of AK fire. No cover, just the solace of mother earth. He has landed in what remains of Lovelace's bunker, which is nothing. Cheng brings up a fistful of mud. How could he have landed in mud—it hasn't rained in days. What he holds looks like strawberry worms in this phosphorescent daylight. He has lost his rifle. He crawls for the nearest cover, which he does not know was his sister's bunker.

The parachutes flare near the ground and pull darkness with them like a black curtain. Red, white tracer rounds cut through the dark; high explosives are thick splashes of white, yellow, red flame; a red haze has risen behind the trees from the burning village.

An NVA mortar round strikes the gasoline stacked against the hillside, and the exploding drums hurtle into the air like catapulted barrels of burning pitch from another era of war. They fly hundreds of feet, explode, light the sky. They land in the village, in the trees on top of the hill, they soar out over the mountaintop and land on the hillside among the NVA, splashing great yellow blossoms of flame.

Shepard fires down the hill. Dead and wounded NVA lie jumbled. The smell of blood and burning flesh and stomach contents and shit mixes with cordite and phosphorus and smoke rolling out of the burning village.

NVA stride up the hill through bodies, over bodies. Some are double-timing. Shepard cuts them down. It is like cutting grass, but the grass keeps growing. Such a number of bodies builds up that the NVA must climb over their dead and wounded comrades. The newly dead reach out with an arm, a leg. Sometimes they sit up. Sometimes, if they died on their stomachs, they hunch their butts in the air like babies.

Shepard pulls out an empty magazine, turns it around, jams in the full magazine taped to it. AK rounds rip the sandbags to his left: The NVA have breached the perimeter, and they are rolling up his flank. Their mortars are ranging in on the bunkers, walking through the forest toward the perimeter like monster footsteps. Air support can't get here in time, and the strike will decimate everything on the mountain anyway. Shepard's face says: *So this is how it ends*. He rises and continues to fire.

SHEPARD
G'bye, Ma. I love ya.

Cheng is curled on the ground as deep into the sandbagged bunker as he can crawl. Fire from the hillside and from the left flank is so heavy that it has begun to topple the sandbags. Cheng realizes that he has no weapon. He is not in uniform. Maybe the Communist troops will see him as a noncombatant. But then why would he be here in a bunker? *Do anything to avoid capture by the Communists. That is not a way you want to die*, Captain Shepard has told them. Cheng doesn't want to die at all. The terror he feels is marrow-deep. He evacuates his bladder. His bowels go. Can he summon the courage to run out and face his death like a Hmong warrior? He rises to his hands and knees, lifts his eyes to the fiery dark.

In the next instant the world explodes. The mountain rises into the air and comes down as its smallest constituent parts: grains of sand, rock, strings of vegetation. Cheng is smashed into the ground and covered in a shell of sandbags.

The F-4s make one more run, unload two more six-bomb racks in the valley and up the hillside, and then they scream away.

ON THE PERIMETER—DAWN

has broken. The destruction left in the wake of the Marine F-4 Phantoms challenges sense and understanding. Nothing larger than a sandbag or a smoking tree trunk remains on the hillside or the mountaintop.

IN THE COLLAPSED BUNKER

Cheng wakes to a different world. He weeps at the beautiful quiet, weeps at the faint dawn he sees through an opening in the jumbled sandbags that saved his life. The smell is something he has dreamed: It is the blood-soaked, flesh-strewn, terror-drenched floor of Ndu Nyong's corral at the end of the world.

Cheng's window is a space between sandbags the size and shape of a loaf of bread.

FROM CHENG'S POINT OF VIEW

skinless, faintly glowing red legs walk on skinless feet. The veins and arteries shimmer with the pulse of Dab blood.

Dab voices ring with good cheer. Happy Dab at play. Dab legs kick at something.

A skinless foot kicks the dark, ovoid thing through Cheng's little window.

IN THE COLLAPSED BUNKER

Cheng bucks, twists, tries to cover his head against the grenade blast. But he can't move. He reaches to throw it back. But he can't grab it. He can only just touch it with the tips of the fingers of one hand.

And he feels that it is not a grenade. It is a silk ball, burnt and misshapen.

FROM CHENG'S POINT OF VIEW

a Dab face appears in the window. It is a ball of bloody yarn with eyes. It is happy. This landscape offers many more toys than a tattered Hmong silk ball. The face goes . . . the legs go. Gentle dawn remains.

IN THE COLLAPSED BUNKER

Moua Cheng plays his fingertips over the patches of unburnt silk and listens for the thump of the choppers like the distant heart of America.

Massage

SONYA SONES

I'm lying on the couch
in the living room,
lying here on my stomach
with my eyes closed,
resting my forehead on my crossed arms,
trying to relax
while Joe rubs my back.

But I can't relax
because Joe's rubbing my back
and he *has* been
ever since I let it slip
that my back was tense
so that he'd get the idea to rub my back
to relax me.

And he's been at it now
for a long lingering while,

x

x

I'm lying on the couch
in the living room,
lying here on my stomach
with my eyes closed,
resting my forehead on my crossed arms,
trying to relax
while Joe rubs my back.

But I can't relax
because Joe's rubbing my back
and he *has* been
ever since I let it slip
that my back was tense
so that he'd get the idea to rub my back
to relax me.

And he's been at it now
for a long lingering while,

just like I dreamed it once,
kneeling over me
with his thighs gently gripping
and his hands so hot that they're
singeing me right through my tee shirt.

Joe's rubbing my back
and my tee shirt's melting away
or maybe his hands are slipping under it
and his fingers
are swirling across my skin now
and sliding so slow,
so oh, oh, oh,

slithering down my shoulders
and wandering along my spine
and I can't relax
because the tips of his fingers
are sizzlingly close to my breasts now
and I'm almost sure he can feel
the softness of the sides of them

and it's all I can do
to keep myself from arching my back
ever so slightly,
and raising up just enough
so that he can
reach under me

and touch them.

It Was Only a Back Rub

None of the other stuff,
the stuff I *wished* would happen,
happened.

Because all of a sudden
Joe's cell phone
started ringing.

Beepy little strains of
"Take Me Out to the Ball Game"
wafted out from the inner recesses of his jeans
and he had to leap up off of me
to dig his Nokia out of his pocket.

I suppose it didn't help matters any
that it was his mother.
And that she was shouting that
he was late to his lunch with his grandmother
and he better get his butt
over there right now.

I guess that sort of nuked the mood.

Because he didn't even try
to kiss me good-bye after that,
not even when I rolled over onto my back,
tossed my hair seductively,
and gazed at him with
the dreamiest bedroom eyes I could muster.

He just gave me an embarrassed smile,
mumbled an apology,
and was out the door
before my pulse even returned to normal.

Later On

My hands
touch
my untouched places,

imagining
how his hands might have felt
on my skin,

trying to feel
how my skin might have felt
to his hands.

Excerpt from

Gone Lonesome

GARY MILLER

The Book of Tongues

CHAPTER 1

It was a Sunday in early March 1952, the end of the first winter after Mama died, and nothing could bring her back. Not the Spirit. Not Jesus. Her body lay in the ground and her soul was in Heaven and a fifteen-year-old boy couldn't change that, even if he was her son. Even if he loved her. That morning, I sat with what was left of us, my father and sisters, my grandfather, on a pew in the Shale Creek Church of the Pentecost and listened to the Reverend Cole tell us how the Lord faced death.

"And Jesus," the reverend said as I looked up from the pew, "when HIS TIME HAD COME!

wasafraid.

"And Jesus," he said, "in HIS TIME OF NEED!
            spoketotheLord.
"And Jesus," he said, "REMINDED US
            thatwecanspeaktoo.
"Let us pray."

The Reverend Cole bowed his head, leaned forward
on the lectern, gripped it with his thick, cow-butcher
hands. The white hairs on his knuckles caught the muted
color from the stained glass windows as he prayed, purple
the robes of the King, red the blood of the Lamb, the
seething spirit fire.

"The world is a FIRE,
            You lead us through, Lord.
"It's a PURIFYING fire,
            but we suffer in its heat.
"We are consumed.
"Let Your VOICE speak through us.
            Let Your HOLY SPIRIT salve us.
"HEAL our wounds
            as You have healed the wounded before us.
"Let us go on."

I bowed my head and tried to pray, but no prayer
came. I didn't want to be healed; I only wanted Mama,
and she was in Heaven. The Angel of Death was sweetly
calling, telling me how easy it would be to die and be
with Mama again. I had a roof beam and a length of rope,
and I'd seen the slipknot and how it was tied. Like Jesus, I
was wounded and afraid. But I couldn't find the words to
cry out to God.

•   •   •

Mama died on November 4, 1951, with her wounds unhealed, alone. I'd walked half a mile up Singers Hollow from our house that morning, to watch a crew on the Ross oil lease drill a new well. My grandfather, Cap Talbot, had taken my sisters into Kendrick to pick up a load of groceries at Ella Johnston's store. My father was working in his welding shop, across the dirt road from the house. I was the one who found her.

I came home in the early afternoon, expecting she'd be in the kitchen, working on supper, listening to the hillbilly gospel music on WRMO radio. But the woodstove was cold and the house was silent. I walked it, room to room.

"Mama." The sound of my voice fell back from the walls with a whispery echo. I called her name louder, and the echo came back just the same.

Her sewing bag sat on the stuff-seated couch in the living room. An old pair of my father's dungarees, patched at the knees and the seat with carefully cut squares of cotton, lay over the couch's arm.

The upstairs rooms were empty. The wind hit the sides of the house, rattled the loose windows. The sound of a hammer beating metal came from the welding shop, muffled by the distance and the wind.

Behind the house was a tool-dressers' shed, where my father's drilling crew had stored their equipment before he went broke sinking dry wells and set up on his own as a welder to fix machines broken in the fields. The shed was abandoned, most of the equipment gone, tins of rusted bolts, broken wooden crates, scrap pipe and buckets of lube grease, broken bottles and coils of inch-thick manila rope left behind. The door leaned on its hinges half open as Mama had left it, its bottom dragging the floor. I squeezed through the gap of it into the dim, oily light.

She hung from the roof beam, a twist of rough manila around her neck, one cloth shoe flung off from her kicking. Shit had run down her calf below the hem of her dress, and her piss puddled below her on the rotted wooden floor. Her arms lay against her sides like the arms of a cloth doll, and her face was black as a plum.

The Reverend Cole stood humped over the lectern, his hands pressed hard against one another, his lips silently working as he read the text to himself. Runnels of sweat slid across his face as he prayed, paused for a moment in the creases of flesh between his cheek and the wide, solid bridge of his nose, and dropped onto the Bible spread open on the lectern. On the wall behind him, high up near the roof beam, the Lord hung dead on a spare wooden cross. The reverend looked up from the lectern and spoke.

"And the Lord said, 'Behold, they are one people, and they have all one language; and this is only the beginning of what they will do; and nothing that they propose to do will now be impossible for them.'

"God gave us our own VOICE,
          and only HE understands it.

"Let the LORD'S voice
          come through you.

"Let the SPIRIT
        take hold of your tongue.
"Speak from your SOUL
        in the voice that He has given you.
"OPEN your hearts, now,
        and speak to the Lord."

The reverend moved hard into it, shouting, singing, beating cadence with his palms, pacing behind the lectern. He carried us, worked us to a thin, sweating rime that mixed with the heavy, dry hot of the cast-iron heat pipes to form an invisible human steam. The sounds of the church carried on the liquid air, the creak of the pews and the warm rumble of prayer, words spoken in praise of the glories of the pure fire of Justice, words raised against the smoking, sulfurous kiln of the Deceiver. And then the words themselves melted in the steam, and other sounds began to break free.

There with Mama in the tool-dressers' shed, I heard the voice of the Angel of Death for the first time. I set up the wooden crate that Mama had stood on when she tied the noose, took out my pocketknife, held the rope in one hand and sawed at it with the other. The rope sang with her weight; the dull, rusted knife slipped and cut across the back of my knuckle and I started to cry. Mama's soft, straw-colored hair was caught up in the rope. I tried to pull it loose and it came out in my hand, stiff and broken.

When the rope gave, her weight took me to the floor on top of her. The wind went out of me and the knife skittered off into a corner. My face lay against hers. Her skin was still warm, and when I rolled off her onto the floor, air pressed out from her lungs with a blunt sound that was nothing like her voice had been when she was alive, and I lay there and covered my head with my hands. I heard a dark rustle of wings then, and a voice softly whispering something I couldn't quite hear. I lifted my hands and looked up, but there was nothing, only the frayed shank of rope still tied around the roof beam.

People began to be taken by the Tongues. Ella Johnston spoke first, a hard, forced *TAH!* from a pew somewhere behind me, then *TAH!* again and *CAMM-TEH-TAH!* her voice powerful for such an old woman, rich and darkly ecstasied, bathed in the Spirit.

The church doors were closed down tight against the weather, and the air that lay in the pews was hot and stank with the smells of salt and tobacco, wet wool and the crude oil the men tracked in on their boot soles. The hard maple pews, worn free of varnish, radiated human smells. Sweat. Spit. Tears. Piss, even, from times when people were so taken up by the Tongues that their soul lifted away with the Spirit, leaving the shells of their bodies behind, jerking and shivering in the pews, out of control.

Cap sat next to me, his hands folded together and resting on the shiny knees of his suit. He swallowed, licked his dark, papery lips and closed his mouth, clamped down hard. The muscles of his jaw swelled and knotted as he worked the Tongues up through his soul, as the Spirit spread throughout his body, and his face darkened with blood until it seemed that he would seize. He raised his hands slowly up to shoulder height and opened his palms, leaned his head back and relaxed, and his whole body joined with the Spirit. His lips hung slack and his mouth fell open and the most beautiful voice came, almost like singing, *HUMALARNAY, HUMALARNAY, KEN SAH HUMALARNAY, HUMALARNAY, KEN SAH*. The deep, full sound resonated in my narrow chest and expanded, filling me with love and with wanting to be close to him. The voice vibrated through me, holy and pure.

I curled in a ball on the floor of the tool-dressers' shed. Then the Angel spoke again, loud enough so I could hear. If I chose to live, I would be without Mama. If I chose to die, I could be with her again, hear her voice and touch her, talk with her and sing with her and listen to her laugh. Mama lived in Heaven now, in eternal life, and I could have that life if I wanted it. The Angel sang to me, soothed me in her warm, dark oil. I felt the soft brush of her wing on my shoulder, closed my eyes and bathed in her darkness. It would be easy. I could throw the rope over the roof beam, the same as Mama had, duck my head into the loop of it, and step away from this earthly world forever.

The coil of rope lay beside Mama on the floor. There was enough for a knot at my throat and another around the roof beam. I drew a tight loop around my neck. The rope nocked in underneath my jaw; the sharp bristle of it burned against my skin. I imagined how Mama had suffered to leave this world, how Jesus had suffered on Calvary, and the burn felt good to me and I drew the rope tighter. I tied a hard knot to the roof beam, and set the wooden crate up on end.

I heard my father's Willys Jeep pull up in front of the house. The doors slammed and I heard the shrieking and laughing of the girls. Rose was five years old then, Marie was three, but already their laughter was so like Mama's, and when I heard those sounds, sweet and familiar, the voice of the Angel was silenced.

I pulled open the rope at my throat and ducked my head from the noose, undid the knot at the roof beam, and flung the rope into the corner. I tried to yell to call them to me, but my voice was empty, and then I was stumbling across the yard and through the back door into the kitchen.

"Mama," I said, finally, and then my voice washed out to nothing, but that was enough. I could see in Cap's and my father's eyes that they knew.

The reverend came down from the pulpit, strode from pew to pew, shouting praise over the Speakers, laying on hands.

"Every MAN that speaks in tongues," he said,
        "Every WOMAN AND CHILD
SPEAKS in the LORD'S voice."

I closed my eyes and tried to feel the Spirit, tried to hear it, but instead I heard the Angel singing. I called her the Angel of Death after a song Hank Williams sang on the hillbilly radio, and as I tried to bring the Spirit up through me, I heard Hank's voice mixing with the Angel's.

Of all the tongues I'd heard speak Jesus, speak God and love, loss and pain, Hank Williams's was the truest, better than any Pentecostal preacher or any other singer I'd ever heard. When Hank sang, I felt like his voice came up inside me, wrapped the joy and sorrow of the world in a blanket around my spine. Hank knew the Lord and he knew the Angel, knew the inside of a liquor bottle and the inside of his soul. When he sang "I Saw the Light," I believed that he really saw Glory. When he sang "Long Gone Lonesome Blues" or "I Heard My Mother Praying for Me," you knew that his misery would dim as much light as he'd ever see. The Reverend Cole tried to tell us what it was like to be Jesus, hanging there on the cross, but Hank sent the answer through his voice. Being Jesus was the part of life that the Lord couldn't save you from.

When Hank sang, I came as close as I could to understanding what had happened to Mama. Before her spells came, it seemed she was always happy, and I wondered how she could always give of herself so much when we had so little, giving help, giving prayers, giving work and even money to the church when I knew that we mostly had none. But when the spells took her I began to wonder, and it plagued me that I hadn't seen it, that there might have been a sadness there all along, not from any cause, other than living.

When I sat by the radio in the front room on Saturday nights listening to Hank Williams sing, that voice told me that I was on the trail of something, that life was

something I'd only begun to feel the hurt of. I imagined
the Angel watching from high up in the rafters, too dark
to be seen, as Hank leaned over the microphone. His
voice came out of the cabinet of the RCA Victor and I
heard every joy and every sorrow that had ever been.
Later, when the Opry was over and the radio turned off, I
listened to the Angel, who told me that since Mama had
gone the joy was for other people only, the rich men like
Basil Ross, the oil driller who owned most of Kane
County, Pennsylvania, and not the poor people like us,
the Mackoways, who lived in a beaten down house in the
Hollow and scratched for what they got. For me, the
world would only be sorrow, and the Angel called me
closer, offered another path, asked me to die.

In the pews of the Shale Creek Church of the Pentecost, the Tongues roiled around me like the wind in a
winter storm. My father held the girls up close to him,
their pale green eyes wide at the noise and the sight of
it, the moaning and chanting and people standing
and swaying, rolling in the pews. My father sat motion-
less, his head bowed. He was raised a Methodist, came to
the Pentecostal church because of Mama, and brought us
there because that is what she would've wanted. He didn't
speak the Tongues.

I closed my eyes and listened to my grandfather, felt
his voice vibrate through me. I tried to build on his
power, tried to squeeze it through my windpipe, to call
the Spirit into me and speak in the Voice of the Lord. In

my lap, my folded hands clenched; the muscles of my stomach pulled until my ribcage burned. I held my breath and tried to drive the Spirit up and out of me—but nothing came.

Behind me, Ella Johnston's voice relaxed as she lay in the arms of the Lord, fell into a quiet, murmurous hum, *camm–teh–tah camm–teh–tah camm–teh–tah camm–teh–tah camm–teh–tah. Camm–teh–tah.* I made a clicking sound with my tongue, let out a weak moan, but the sounds were false and unholy, made by my own small self and not the Lord, just as they had been every time I'd tried.

For some reason I couldn't understand, I'd been denied the Spirit. Even as a young boy, I was fascinated by the stories the preachers told about being taken by the Fire, having the Word of the Lord pass through our mouths. I watched with awe on Sunday mornings as people spoke the Tongues, and they seemed to me the most beautiful sound I'd ever heard. I talked with Mama about it again and again.

"What's it like to get the Tongues?" I'd say. "How does it feel?"

"It's like bein' filled up with goodness," she'd say. "Hope. When I get to feelin' like this place is godforsaken, the Spirit tells me it's not. It holds me up. It tells me it'll be all right till somethin' better comes along."

"Is it Jesus?"

"Partly."

"What more, then?"

"It's nothin' I can explain."

"I want to get the Spirit," I said.

"We all do, honey. Can't nothin' else save us but the power to speak."

HUMALARNAY, HUMALARNAY, KEN SAH; HUM-ALARNAY, HUMALARNAY, KEN SAH; HUMALAR-NAY, HUMALARNAY, KEN SAH; HUMALARNAY, HUMALARNAY, KEN SAH.

Ecstasies churned the air. Reverend Cole stopped his pacing, froze, squeezed the edges of the lectern in his hands until the pressed wood popped. He stared hard into the rafters, sweat darkening the neck of his robe, a spray of it leaping when he shook his head. His mouth jagged open and the dark velvet nap of his tongue pulsed in the seat of his jaw. He shouted out over the congregation:

AHALNA, SUMITSCAR, RUMING BONN
TAMISS TAMISS HARRIA
RANN HACCA COMMALALNTICA HAR

I turned and saw other Speakers, a young woman kneeling backward in the pew and moaning, a whole family of farmers from Pine Shanty, man and wife and sons and daughters standing, their tallowy faces washed in shadow-blue light from the stained glass. Voices lifted from the darker pews in the back corners. The Tongues melded into a warm buzz.

I watched them, listened and wondered if the Spirit could save them all, if their faith was strong enough. Mama had ended up hanging on a rope, and I wondered if it had been her lack of faith, as some people whispered, and if so, how she felt that Jesus had let her down, or God, or both, whom she had been so faithful to since I'd been old enough to know about such things. It seemed strange to me that she had listened instead to the Angel, who said that faith was being close to the Lord and that death meant being in the Lord's arms.

CAMM-TEH-TAH, HUMALARNAY, HUMALAR-NAY, KEN SAH; HUMALARNAY, HUMALARNAY, KEN SAH; CAMM TAMISS TAMISS HARRIA TEH TAMISS TAMISS HARRIA TAH RANN HACCA COM-MALALNTICA HAR.

Only the Lord could keep me from the Angel. As much as I wanted to go with her, as much as I wanted to die, I still wanted the Spirit, and in the roaring of the Tongues, I cried out to Him.

"Oh Jesus," I begged, "come to me! Jesus, speak through me! Jesus bathe me with the Spirit fire. Oh," *Mama* (I didn't say this), *Oh, Mama, how did that rope feel against your throat; how did the stink of grease and gasoline, the thick black air of the tool-dressers' shed fill up your nose? Wasn't there something else you wanted than that? Isn't there a natural way to die? The Angel sits on my shoulder, folds me in her wings and sings to me in tongues like the lonesome music from the hillbilly radio, and she is with me and asking me to go to the Lord, and oh, her voice is so sweet.*

Suddenly the door of the church flew open. Suddenly the sunlight roared in, and the wind came and the smell of rain and life, sweeping the sweat and saliva, the human stink, out into the air, and the church was cleansed and the church fell silent and the Spirit was lost and the faces came back and the people stood, sweat-soaked, panting, blinking in the sharp light, and the weight of the Angel was lifted from my shoulder, and the loneliness was gone, and the black silhouette of a boy stood in the doorway, and in a small, scared voice, he spoke.

"They told me to come get you. Them up on the Farris lease. There's a accident, and they need the men."

CHAPTER 2

The bulldozer rested upright on its left track fifty yards below the muddy lease road, the path from where it hit the boulder and rolled marked by deep, ruddy gouges in the hillside, by the fresh white of the bark-stripped and broken saplings that it mangled as it fell. The smell of diesel hung in the air. The cooling engine hissed and ticked as the raindrops struck it. Men huddled in small groups across the side hill, speaking quietly or not at all; they stood some distance off from the dozer, as if taking time to let their feelings settle. Underneath the machine, Alton Spence's boy Donny lay dead.

The rain drove down heavy and had turned cold; it beat on the outside of my black rubber rain cape and soaked my dungarees through where they stuck out below it; the cold numbed my fingers so that I could hardly keep hold of the rough manila rope. Gum Kent had hooked two heavy lines at the top side of the dozer, one at the back end and one at the blade, swung the lines around the hips of two big maple trees further down the hill and back up to where all of us stood.

I stood next to my father impatient for all of it to begin, churning up mud with the toe of my boot.

"What's he waitin' for?" I said. "Why don't he just give the word?"

"You in a hurry to see this, are you?" my father said. He pulled his red wool cap down level with his rusty eyebrows, blinked the water from his rain-colored eyes.

"No sir," I said, "I'm just freezin', is all," but that was a lie. I'd been with death once before, and bad as it had been and still was, in my daytime mind and my dreams, I wanted to be with it again. The feeling of wanting it drifted into me, as if I could scent on the idea of it like a dog would, and it tingled inside me, like tiny fires under my skin. Donny Spence was lying dead under the dozer, and it wasn't right for me to want to be so near, but if I could be with death again, maybe I wouldn't be afraid. I'd be able to use the rope in the tooldressers' shed, slip it around my throat for real this time, step off the edge of the upturned crate and be with Mama again.

There on the hillside, with the rain getting colder and threatening sleet, I closed my eyes and tried to hear her voice, the way she sang when WRMO played the hillbilly gospel music, the high, open joy of it all, as if nothing could be better than this world. But just when I coaxed out the first sweet notes from my memory, other sounds came. Mama talking when a spell ruled her tongue, low and angry and spitting words like she couldn't get them out of her mouth fast enough. The bitter, sparking sounds that lingered in the darkness of our front porch, our kitchen, our upstairs hall. I flung my eyes open to chase the sounds away.

Gum stood further down the hill, just above the dozer. He cupped his hands to his face and shouted. His voice boomed like a drill motor, and steam tumbled from his hands. "I'll raise up my arms. When I drop 'em back down, you pull. Whatever you do, don't wrap your hands up in them lines. Once that dozer gets movin', she'll take you right on with her."

A dozen or so men walked toward us, joined us on the rope. A dozen more formed a second column, thirty feet away. Through the heavy rain, I picked out the faces of the men who'd come to carry Mama away.

At the time Mama died, we had no telephone, so my father ran down Singers Hollow to Harold Hanks's place to use his. Harold, who owned a little drilling outfit that my father did welding for, drove his pickup back up the Hollow and parked it in our yard, helped my father into the house and down onto the stuff-seated sofa in our living room.

"Do you want me to take a blanket out there?" Harold said.

My father began to cry then; long, loping whines that rattled my eardrums and made me shiver with fear. Daddy had never acted this way, even when Mama was at her worst. He seemed less afraid of her than anyone I could picture, except maybe for Cap, and I remember wondering how he could do it, hold so steady and fearless while such strangeness held Mama in its grip. But now he was sobbing, and it terrified me.

"It won't be twenty minutes before they're here with the ambulance," Harold Hanks said. "You fellas just tell me what you want till then, and I'll do it."

Take your truck off our yard, I wanted to say. *It don't belong there. Put my mother back alive.* But then I thought of Mama alone. I went to the kitchen and drew a glass of water, slipped out the back door to the tool-dressers' shed.

Sitting in the darkest corner of the shed I watched over her. Her face looked swollen even with the rope cut loose. I could taste the shit smell in the air, hear my sister Marie crying up in her room, the sound like the tinning of a far-away radio.

Harold came to the door and stood for a moment. I watched him peer through the doorway gap, bending at the waist, his long, skinny hands tucked into the front pockets of his dungarees. He leaked out a sigh. "Jesus, Katherine," he said, and I waited for him to say something else, that Mama was crazy like plenty of people had said and meant, or if it was just plain terrible of her to leave her family behind this way, but he didn't. Instead, he leaned against the door and forced it back open, and the light fell on her face and fooled me for just that moment into thinking that she was still alive, that she might catch me up in her arms and kiss me like she did when I was a little boy, singing songs along with the radio in a voice like an angel's. And then I made out the ripened bruise at her throat and started to cry, and Harold noticed me there in the dark. He was a very tall man and he squatted down, and his hard, narrow face showed kindness.

"I thought you was supposed to be in the house," he said. He put his hand on my shoulder, helped me up, moved me out the door and across the yard toward the house.

"I want to talk to her for a minute."

"Not right now. Later. When she's cleaned up, and you can see her how she was before. Now go on in the house with your dad and your grampa."

Harold tried to stop me, but I pushed around him and twisted out of his hands, ran back across the yard to the tool-dressers' shed. As I knelt on the oil-soaked floor, the Angel whispered, told me how peaceful it would be if I joined Mama in Heaven, and I tried to ignore that soothing voice, so I could tell Mama everything, how much I loved her, how sad it made me to see her there on the floor with one of her favorite dresses ruined, how afraid I was to be alone in the world without her.

I said a word or two and the Angel's words returned then, whispers at first, and then louder, startling me into silence, mixing with my thoughts until I couldn't make sense of either. The room took on a dimness, then began to drag down to dark, and it may have been minutes and it may have been an hour when Harold came back into the shed to get me.

"Come on, now," he said. He hooked his arms under my own and across my chest, and dragged me back to the house. I watched from the window of my bedroom while the men from the Kendrick town ambulance walked out to the shed, businesslike at first, unafraid but then slowing as they stepped across the yard, until they eased through the crooked-leaning door with the kind of hesitating I felt sometimes when I entered the Shale Creek chapel and it was empty or almost so. It was twenty minutes or better when they finally carried her body from the tool-dressers' shed to where the ambulance waited, nosed up into the yard next to Harold Hanks's pickup truck. Kenny Wright and Louis Whiteman carried the stretcher, with Mama laid on it beneath a sheet. I couldn't raise a whisper to say good-bye to her even then.

For a week after she died, people came. Fred Hanks, Harold's older brother, nailed the door to the tool-dressers' shed closed. John Francis split up a load of firewood for us, and went home and got his wife, Sarah, who brought other women with their casseroles and loaves of homemade bread, dust rags and mop buckets. They talked to my sisters and held them on their laps, sang to them and told them stories, but the women's voices were different from Mama's voice, and Mama's voice was gone.

It was then that I began to understand how perfect a voice could be, how unto itself and itself only, common in some ways, but peculiar to only one person, and how when someone died their voice died with them, and never made another sound. For most of the week that followed, I stayed in my room in a chair by the window, looked down onto the tool-dressers' shed, where, high up in the roof beams, the coiled manila rope hung, waiting.

Gum looked up toward us and raised his hand. You could tell by the way he leaned into the hill that he was half drunk.

"There's somebody to look up to," my father said, speaking quietly so that only I could hear, pretending he was talking to himself. "Somebody to spend your spare time with."

I took a better grip on the rope, but didn't answer. Gum Kent had been a fixture on the oil leases since he was my age, years before I was born. And since I was a tiny boy, I'd been drawn to him. His dark, wooly beard, his bearishness and toothless smile scared some people, but made me feel warm and wanted somehow, in a way that no one else did.

When I was young, I didn't understand that Gum drank too much liquor, or maybe he didn't back then, but by the time I was old enough to spend time with him on my own, I saw the truth of it. Gum drank morning, night, and in between, during work and after. He could do the work of three men, and drink the whiskey of them, too. My father had always tried to keep me away from him, as if just being around Gum Kent was enough to make me become him. But I didn't count the drinking as a problem. Gum always treated me decent, and talked to me man-to-man, which was something my father could never seem to do, even before Mama died.

Halfway down the slope, Gum dropped his hand, and

we began to pull. The rope stung tight, spat shards of rain along its length, and we dug our boots into the mud and leaned. The roar of the rain filled my ears; when the dozer began to fall, the noise of its shifting cleats, the snapping over of the last small saplings that held it upright, reached me dully. Even when Gum yelled for us to drop the lines, even when the dozer tumbled the rest of the way down the slope, snapping off trees and ripping at the dirt, spraying cordwood-sized chunks of sod, it seemed to take place without sound. Only the rain and the beat of the distant powerhouse motors filled up the spaces between the trees. My father tried to lead me back to the Willys, but I couldn't stop myself from looking at what I was half-afraid to see.

Donny Spence's body was mangled into a muddy gash in the side of the hill. One of his legs doubled back on itself, the bone of the thigh jagged out through a tear in his dungarees. His rib cage was flattened. A pinkish froth leaked from his mouth onto the soil. The rain fell.

Kenny Wright took off his slicker and covered the body over. Arthur Lewis and Fred Carrollton brought a long, narrow piece of plywood nailed to two-by-fours for a stretcher. They lifted Donny onto it and carried him uphill to the road, laid him out on the wooden flatbed of Harold's Chevy pickup.

The rain had stopped suddenly, and the woods seemed unearthly quiet. We made a circle around the body where it lay on the rough-hewn planks and took off our hats. The Reverend Cole's words smoked from his mouth in the chill air.

"Lord, this boy is lost to us here, but he rests in your

arms in Heaven. And sure as we know that, it pains us to wonder why. Speak to our hearts. Tell us why you chose him, and why you chose us to stay behind."

I listened for God's answer and heard nothing. As the Reverend Cole continued to pray, I turned my head away.

At the outskirts of the prayer circle stood a tall, skinny man in a black wool pea coat and dungarees, a black wool watch cap. Between his turned-up coat collar and the bottom edge of the cap was flour–white skin topped by thick, loose hanks of sooty black hair. Then the man moved closer, reached up with a pale white hand, and pulled off the watch cap, and I saw that he was not a man at all, but a girl. With the cap removed, her hair escaped completely, spilled like oil down around her shoulders, blacker even than the wool of her coat. Her black eyes held an oily shine as well; her nose was slight, her lips dark as sumac berries, even with the cold.

"I'm Dorothy Spence," she said into the silence after the reverend stopped praying. "He's my brother, and I'll take him. You don't have to worry about no ambulance— or no coroner, either." Her voice was clear and sweet and sure of itself, and I wondered how she could be so calm when her brother had died this way.

"Alton's in the car," she said. "If you help me get Donny in the backseat, we'll take him over to the funeral home in Kendrick." She pointed to a rusty white Rambler, parked fifty yards down the road. A few of the men looked expectantly toward the Rambler, and she shook her head. "He's passed out in the front. I'd as soon let him be."

The reverend nodded. He came forward and took her

in his arms, kissed her on the forehead. It was then that she started to cry.

"I'm sorry," the reverend said, as if he knew that saying it was close to saying nothing. He stood for a moment with his mouth open, his tongue slowly moving but making no sound.

"I know it," she said. "And sorry's enough to be for now." She raised her head, and the tears were gone, as quickly as they'd come. She stepped forward to the back of the truck and pulled back the slicker, touched her brother's face. She bent and softly kissed his forehead.

"It's all right, Donny," she said. "I'm here to take you with me now, and you don't have to worry." She folded the rain slicker back over him and stepped away.

Arthur Lewis and the Reverend Cole carried Donny Spence to the car, laid him on the backseat and closed the door. Dorothy got behind the wheel, and the motor choked and caught. She slammed the door and dropped the car into gear. As the Rambler pulled away, Alton Spence rose up on his seat, stared until the car sank down below the lip of the hill and into Singers Hollow. A white gauze of exhaust smoke rose in the wet air. I stood in the middle of the road, watching until the smoke disappeared.

Terror

R. GREGORY CHRISTIE

The Terror Class

ELIZABETH LORDE-ROLLINS

I.

They'd had three before her
the suburban sacrifice
fresh from Spence on the East Side
the knives surprised her
and she never did hang up
the Smurf display of fractions
she'd brought to entertain them
instead of Saturday morning cartoons
she found Saturday night specials
ten-year-olds cutting
each other in the halls
she started to wonder if she'd been wrong
were they worth saving
they might have saved her from her ignorance

but she talked all the time, she had
so much to teach
the first time she hit a child
Kesha smiled at the familiar grip
go on and hit me Kesha yelled
bitter drip from fifth grade lips
it won't matter bitch
they call us the terror class

II.

We're the terror class
I'm dangerous when grown
does my bebop scare you
yeah
I'm not snot in your educated nostrils,
    mothafucka
so stop picking at me
others bring their limp-ass guilt
in with the morning coffee
their shallow Long Island smiles
certainly don't put the milk
in my cornflakes
everyone knows we don't matter
no one will be there to tell the grinch
take your hands off my child
welfare money means you have to stay
good and quiet for Form 407
no one is gonna make a fuss
when your teachers deposit

their rage in the circular file
that is your mind.

Training begins at 8:40
the Black woman principal
somebody's mama
stands dripping Dior
says
I don't know why these Black people
don't move out of Harlem
valedictorian of the terror class.

III.

Me and Rodney was buddies
used to hang
started in second grade
teacher made me cry for drawing on my work
    folder
I just wanted to show her
what multiplication looked like
In sixth grade Rodney discovered
the quickest rising bread
comes in crack
and fell in with Rufus,
big, sixteen, and four years outta school already.
So one night Rodney pantin at my door
says, man, you gots to hole this fuh me
I be back fo it
he never looked so funky

like he ain't been home in four days.
That night I dream the drip from the ceiling
is pouring blood instead of rustwater
and Rodney he don't come to school no more.
Next week, I'm coming from ball I see
Rodney's mama cryin in the street
super found him at the bottom of the elevator
    shaft
been dead a week but they knew it was him
Rufus got it so made he left the heavy chain
"RODNEY" in gold
around that young brotha's neck.
I go home.
I opened the brown bag Rodney gave me
funny I never wanted to see it before
school was useful fuh one thing
I sure learned how to count my money
all twenny thousan of it that night
somewhere Rufus be lookin fuh money
Rodney's body didn't give up.

IV.

Did low-hanging sky past the 155th St. bridge
brand that cloud around your eyes
where did they slip you into cut-down possibility
snuck it in between the cotton cap and your new
    skull
injected it when you had to see your mama beg
the landlord for just one more month

she could put it together with just
a little more time
you need more time?!
why are you so slow, spend your time chewing
    gum
these laaazy children!
first grade memories of school days
SMACK! dear old golden rule days
you, bent even further over the paper
trying to get the letters to stop swimming

Did you die a little
while I pacified your wired daddy
open school day couldn't stop him
from having a little blow before he came over
we got all kinds of powder here
Black minds en polvo are just
instant coffee for the school board
The Spence wonder has already resigned her
    class
graduated to tricyclics
and even my eyes grow dull
stare out from square iron-barred windows
protecting the teachers' lounge
hiding from the assistant principal
we're keeping an abuse file on.

In seven Septembers
will I, too, be training your self-destruction

like a curl, bent and smoothed
a little killing every day?
teach you just say no
to visions before you get to junior high
that is my real job and
what am I doing here
baby, baby don't hope
don't break my heart
you're in the terror class

V.

Does my bebop scare you?
Walking with my buddies
Can I make you cross to the other side
Hey, white bread
Do you resent bein' terrorized
On streets we both know
Belong to you?
If you pull a gun, baby
Do you think you'll pull some time?
If you rape my grandma
Mother, sister, daughter, lover
The cop will grin
When he asks you fuh the juicy details
If he wasn't there
Hey, man
You tell me
Who is the terror class?

FORM 407: an attendance form that must be presented to case-workers in order to receive welfare checks. One form for each school-age child must be presented.

EN POLVO: Spanish, meaning "ground," commonly used with reference to spices.

Intrinsic Value

ALEX FLINN

Mr. Barnes isn't at graduation, of course. Nor Elizabeth. I wish I could say I feel bad about that, but I don't. I look out over the sea of Palm-Aire graduates in flat, black hats, knowing what they think of me. But it isn't because of what happened. Not really. They'd always thought that about me. What happened just gave them a concrete reason to think so.

Doesn't matter. After today, I'm gone, getting what I've always wanted, which is out of here. I'll never see them again.

I step up to the podium.

"It's not fair when you think about it," I said to Lewis while we stood at the intersection the first day back after Christmas break. "Just because you're a guy and can throw a ball, they'll talk to you—even though you live west of the highway."

The light changed, and we dashed to cross U.S. 1—or "the Great Divide" as I liked to call it—the highway that separated the condo development where Lewis and I lived from the palatial estates where all the other inmates of Palm-Aire High School resided. As usual, the light didn't stay green long enough to cross all six traffic lanes. Lewis stopped on the median, grabbing my hand when I tried to go on. He held me there.

"Careful."

So we stood there. A few charitable souls honked, and Lewis said, "My dad likes to tell how he walked miles through the snow, going to school. I guess this is the Florida equivalent of that, huh?"

I didn't have time to nod. The light had gone green again, and we ran the rest of the way across, my hair coming out of its ponytail and blowing all over my face.

I should have envied Lewis, having a dad at home. But if I wasted time envying everyone who had something I didn't have—well, I wouldn't have much time for anything else. So I tried to devote my life to doing something about it instead. My plan: Get good grades, get a scholarship. And get out.

We stopped running, and Lewis said, "Now what shit were you talking before?"

"I said because you're a baseball star, people at school will speak to you despite your being address-impaired—living on the wrong side of the proverbial tracks. But me, I'm just smart, which apparently counts for nothing."

Lewis gave me a look until I added, "Not that you're not smart."

"Oh, no, of course I'm smart. Only reason I'm not second in the class like you is, I been hit by too many baseballs." We reached the actual tracks, and Lewis turned to walk next to them. I stepped on the railroad ties, sometimes touching Lewis's shoulder for balance. "Problem is, Girl Wonder, you're usurping their territory."

"Ten points for *usurping*," I said. I'd started giving Lewis mental points for using a word from the SAT vocabulary list we were studying. "And what do you mean?"

"I mean, they can handle having me around because I act like a poor boy's expected to."

"Meaning?"

"I help their sports teams and don't take up no space in their honors English classes or nothing."

I winced at the triple negative, then realized Lewis was screwing with me.

"You," he continued, "are taking up chairs they feel are rightfully theirs."

"Meaning when a girl like Elizabeth Barnes makes a five-point-five, they're okay with it, but when I do, I'm a threat?"

"Exactly." We reached the Snapper Bay condos where Lewis and I both lived. A haze of dust and mediocrity pervaded the air. Our development was the only property west of the highway districted into Palm-Aire High, so people thought Lewis and I were lucky to go to Palm-Aire. What luck! If I'd gone to Killian, I'd likely have been a shoo-in for valedictorian. Last year's Killian first-in-class had a 4.9. Me, I had a 5.578, and unless Elizabeth Barnes decided to drop out of school and work at McDonald's, the best I could do was second place, which really sucked because I needed, needed, *needed* a full-ride scholarship to go to the college of my choice. The admissions counselor had let me know it was pretty competitive, but being valedictorian would pretty much clinch it for me. Without that, we'd see.

And, more than that, I *wanted* to be valedictorian. Just to show them I could be.

"On the other hand," Lewis was saying, "you don't exactly see the captain of the cheerleading squad doing her splits on my doorstep." He gestured to that doorstep, like, *are you coming in?* which was nice because he knew I always did. "You could probably get a date with anyone you want."

"If I put out, I could," I said, following him inside.

"I'd put out, and it don't do me any good."

I laughed and collapsed onto the sofa. Lewis's place was clean and smelled like Glade PlugIns air freshener.

"That's different. Any girl—any decent-looking girl can get laid any time by pretty much any guy she wants."

"That so?"

"It is indeed so. Because guys are naturally hornier."

"Guys think with their . . ."

"Genitals?" I prompted him. "Yeah."

"So you're saying you could just walk up to any guy and get busy with him?"

"Pretty much."

"Right." Lewis started for the television, but I blocked

him. One of the few benefits of living in this *hole de hell*
was free cable, and Lewis could have watched it pretty
much continuously if you let him. But he needed to keep
up his grades to play spring ball *and* he had to get at least
a 900 on the SAT to be able to accept the athletic scholarship that already had his name on it.

"Care to place a little wager on that?" he asked.

"On what?" Thinking he meant the television.

"What you said. About how you could have any guy
you want."

I opened my AP Statistics book and pointed to Lewis's
business math text. "Right, Lewis. That is just so *Cruel
Intentions*"—which was this dumb teen movie we'd rented
the month before, where this girl bets her stepbrother he
can't lay this other girl. How realistic and relevant to our
lives.

"I was kidding anyway," Lewis said, opening the math
book and leaning close. "You know the only guy I want
you to sleep with is me."

"Aw, Lewis." I smiled and nudged him away. "I'd never
do it with you. You're maybe the only guy around here I
actually *like*."

Mom was sleeping on the sofa (which she'd once again
neglected to open up) when I got home from Lewis's, and
the place smelled like beer and cigarettes. At least she was
alone. I liked it that way, but it was a rarity. Mom had
been shooting for Prince Charming most of my life. She
just had incredibly bad aim. By the time I started getting
used to the guys who smacked her around or moved in

for six months without contributing for rent, she started with a new breed: "nice" guys who paid their share but thought that entitled them to walk around in a bathrobe with nothing underneath. Her reaction when I was thirteen and she found out her boyfriend Richard had been messing with me was to scream and yell (at me!) and put me on the pill.

When that happened, it was like something inside me changed. Before then, I was a little girl, feeling little girl emotions. Things could hurt me then. After, it was like a shield of ice had been placed over my heart. The only thing that could hurt me now was failure.

Mom didn't have a boyfriend now, and I sort of hoped that might last until the end of the school year. When I got that final transcript, I'd be out of there. I didn't care if I had to hitch to college.

I was almost to my room when Mom stirred.

"Where you been?" she asked.

"Lewis's. We were studying."

"That what they calling it these days? You better stay on the pill. We don't need no brown babies."

"Right, Mom." I didn't bother to explain. I headed for my room and opened my history notebook. It was going to be another long night.

A person could almost have felt sorry for Elizabeth Barnes. Almost. True, she was more one of *them* than I was, but not much more. She lived east of the highway, because her mother—who left when sweet Liz was two— apparently paid *mucho dinero* in child support. But her father was Mr. Barnes, the world's nerdiest English teacher, and that is saying A Lot. And Elizabeth herself was a mess.

Like right now, she was still working on an Economics test the rest of us had finished ten minutes before. Her pen moved slowly, writing her essay exactly one word at a time. I counted to ten, knowing what was coming. Sure enough, the second I hit ten, Liz dropped the pen and dove into the fetal position, holding her head and rocking back and forth. It was a ritual she did, like the God of Incredible Dorkiness was going to give her the answers. It used to make me nervous, like I'd forgotten something. But now, there was no doubt in my mind that I was smarter than Elizabeth. I'd matched her, subject for subject, *A* for *A* since tenth grade. It was only in ninth that she got ahead when they put me in dummy regular chemistry while Elizabeth got into an honors class that was supposed to be only for tenth graders. I could have aced that class. Anyone else's mother would have pitched a fit and gotten her daughter into it, but not mine. So that year, I got four points for an *A* in regular, while Elizabeth got five for an *A* in honors. But for that, our GPAs were identical.

"Finished, Elizabeth?" Ms. Perez said, hopefully. She had to know she wasn't.

Elizabeth stopped rocking. "N-no. There are still ten minutes left."

"I just thought..." Ms. P looked at the rest of us, ossifying with boredom. "That's fine, dear."

Elizabeth wrote for the full ten minutes. She handed in her paper at the bell.

Later, I saw her out in the hallway in the English wing with her father.

"How'd the big econ exam go?" he was asking.

"Piece of cake," she said.

"Well, of course," he said. "You're the best." And they high-fived.

No. I didn't feel sorry for Elizabeth. She acted like she made it on her own, but really, she had her father helping her out. I never had anyone to help me.

"I've decided to take you up on your offer," I told Lewis after school that day. I was a little late getting there because we were wrapping up the yearbook—of which I was editor (I'd wanted to be editor of the newspaper, but Elizabeth got that).

"What offer?" Lewis pulled his eyes away from the Cartoon Network a second.

"The wager we discussed yesterday."

Lewis looked puzzled a moment. "Oh, you mean, where I pay you to sleep with some guy. I was shitting you. I don't think my ego could take that."

"Oh." I nodded. "Okay."

I turned off the television and we began doing homework. A minute later, Lewis said, "Okay, I give. Who's the guy?"

"I guess I won't tell you . . . since you aren't interested."

We got back to homework.

A minute later, he said, "So, you're not doing it . . . I mean, without the bet?"

I finished working a trig problem before I answered.

"I'm not sure yet," I said, though I was. "Sometimes, you don't need to be compensated for doing something. Sometimes, things just have intrinsic value."

"What's that mean?"

"It means natural value. If something is intrinsically valuable, you don't need a reward for doing it. It is its own reward."

When Lewis tried to bring it up again, I changed the subject.

It would be easy, I realized Monday in English class. I'd seen him, looking at girls before, so many times. I don't know if I would have done it if I hadn't seen him doing that. I'd heard people say it was disgusting, him looking at girls his daughter's age or even younger. But I understood: He was lonely. I knew what it was to be lonely in this place. Really, it would be a win-win proposition, him and me. We'd each be getting something we needed so bad.

He'd never really looked at me that way. But that day, I dressed not in my usual jeans and sweatshirt, but like the girls I'd seen him noticing. I wore one of Mom's miniskirts and a white blouse with a heart-shaped neckline, left over from a summer waitressing job I'd had. I sat in the front row, as usual, ankle crossed over ankle.

And, halfway through class, I raised my hand.

"Why would Matthew Arnold use a word like *anodyne*?" I asked. "I mean, no reader is going to know what it means."

He walked across the room and paused before me. "Do you know?"

A few people giggled, but I smiled. "Of course. I looked it up." I leaned back in my chair, stretching, both my hands running through my hair. "It means, something which soothes or gives...relief." He was standing before me, looking, like he did, and I said, "Right?"

"Right."

"But that's my point. If even smart people have to look up a word, it disrupts the flow of the poem. Don't you think?"

He was looking, and I ran my tongue across my lips. I felt the tension, almost physical, between us, like a kite one of Mom's boyfriends had gotten me once, and flown when the wind was too strong. I think the others felt it too, and Mr. Barnes. At least, he didn't answer my question, just stammered and went on with his lecture.

But I couldn't do anything about it that day. I had a meeting after school, what I'd hoped would be a quick yearbook one, but no one wanted to take orders from me. They thought they knew better even though none of them had wanted to be editor.

But Tuesday. Definitely Tuesday.

"You coming over after school?" Lewis broke away from his posse of jock friends to talk to me after lunch the next day.

"Maybe late. I have a meeting."

"I thought yearbook was done for a while?"

"It is. I need some extra help in English."

"Yeah, right." Lewis looked disappointed, but I knew that in a few weeks, baseball practice would begin, and I'd be all alone after school anyway.

"I'll come later," I said.

Bryant Walton was approaching Lewis. He was one of those guys who thought he was something because he drove a Miata, but he only pulled passing grades because of Daddy's money and playing football. As I walked away, I heard him say, "She's a hot piece. You doing her?"

"Nah." Lewis sort of laughed. "We're friends."

"Why would you be friends with *her*?" Bryant said. "She's nobody."

I didn't stick around for Lewis's answer.

After class that day, I approached Mr. Barnes's desk. He was fumbling in his drawer for something, and I stared at the thready hairs on the top of his head.

"Mr. Barnes?"

I waited, leaning forward on the flats of my hands like a cat about to spring.

"Yes, er . . ." He looked up, stammering like he'd forgotten my name. I'd worn one of Mom's blouses, and his eyes lingered on my breasts.

"I was wondering . . ." I looked him in the eye. He wasn't that old, not like people thought. His eyes were young. He must have had Elizabeth when he was in college. "I wondered if I could come in after school to discuss the Matthew Arnold assignment?"

Surprise creased his eyebrows. "Well . . . of course. But it hardly seems necessary."

"What do you mean?"

"Nothing. I mean, I just meant you're a good student."

I tilted my head sideways, feeling my hair on my bare shoulder. "I'm a good student because I keep up with my work. But if you're too busy to see me..."

I turned away, pouting. But I didn't leave yet. I waited. "No."

Mr. Barnes was standing, reaching for me.

"No, of course you can come. I'd love to discuss Matthew Arnold with you."

He smiled, a peace offering.

"After school then." My own smile was like anodyne, and I ran off to lunch.

"I think Arnold is saying that people are alienated from one another and from themselves," I said. I read:

> *But we, my love! doth a like spell benumb;*
> *Our hearts, our voices;*
> *Must we too be dumb?*

Mr. Barnes had been sitting at his desk when I came in, so I had to decide whether to sit down or stand at his desk. I finally decided to sit. A few minutes into the conversation, he moved to a student desk beside me, and I knew I'd decided right.

"But he also thought lovers should reveal themselves to each other," he said.

> *Alas, is even Love too weak*
> *To unlock the heart and let it speak?*

Are even lovers powerless to reveal
To one another what indeed they feel?

"Is that true?" I asked.

"Well . . ." He laughed. "That's what it says in the Teacher's Guide."

I laughed too. "No, about lovers not talking to each other?"

"Why ask me?"

I looked at his white, freckled hand on the textbook and made the plunge. "I just thought maybe you knew more about love than I do."

He took the ball. "Pretty girl like you. You've probably been in love dozens of times."

"No . . ." I leaned my chin on my hand, fingertip in mouth. "I barely even have friends. People my age feel threatened by me. Especially boys my age."

He nodded. "Liz says the same thing. You two should talk."

"Yeah." *Whoa . . . not what I wanted.* "But it's different for me. Elizabeth . . . I mean, the others come from the same place, nice families. I'm not like them. I'm alone. No one really notices what I do."

He nodded again, and I added, "I guess that's why I wasn't totally honest with you today, when I said I needed help with the assignment. It wasn't really that so much as . . . I wanted to talk about it."

He looked concerned. "About what?"

"All of it. The poem, poetry, the English language. It's

all so incredible, and no one understands. If I tried to talk to Mom about Matthew Arnold, she'd just laugh at me. But you..." I shook my head.

"What?"

"You just seem like someone I could talk to. I'm sorry. I know it's wrong to take up your time like this. You probably have a wife or girlfriend to get home to."

"No." He shook his head. "I'm alone too, pretty much. I mean, there's Elizabeth, but she's so busy with her own friends these days."

The clock clicked, moving from 3:59 to 4:00.

"So you wouldn't mind if I came to talk to you sometimes?"

I held my breath. If he had a brain in his balding head, he'd suggest I join the English Club, and it would be over.

But he said, "Of course. I've enjoyed our talk."

I smiled, but my brain was racing. I knew tomorrow would be too soon. And Thursday, I had a National Honor Society meeting—I was vice president. (Guess who was president.) So I said, "Friday?"

"I'd like that."

I gathered my books, feeling his eyes boring holes in my back as I left.

In the next two months, I went to see Mr. Barnes after school several times, going from sitting at the student desk to bringing an extra chair up beside him. We talked about poetry, my family, my dreams. We never touched. He mentioned Elizabeth one more time, but the more I went, the more personal our conversations became.

One time, I asked him, "Did you always want to be an English teacher?"

He smiled. "I wanted to be a poet, which is why I'm an English teacher."

"Why not be a poet?"

"I'm not very good . . . as I realized after the hundredth rejection letter."

I leaned toward him, my hair grazing his face. "I hear it's hard to sell poetry."

"Maybe you're right. Maybe I just didn't try hard enough."

"I'd love to read your poems someday."

So from then on, he brought me poems, horrible sonnets with rhymes like *September* and *remember*, stories of lost dreams that I encouraged him to send to magazines.

I never visited more than twice a week. Once, I stayed away for eleven days straight. On the twelfth day, he put his hand on my shoulder after class.

"Is something wrong?" he asked.

"No. Why?" But I knew.

"I just . . . I didn't see you last week at all. I had a few rejection letters, and I . . ." His hand was still on my shoulder. "I wanted to see you."

I waited a second before saying, "I wanted to see you too, Mr. Barnes."

He looked stricken. "I told you to call me Tom."

"Tom. I just worried it wasn't right, me taking so much of your time."

"I *want* to see you. I . . ." His voice trailed off.

"What?"

"I miss you," he said. "I feel like you're the only person I can really talk to."

I didn't answer, and he said, "I'm sorry. I know it's wrong. You're a student."

"No," I said, feeling the warm wetness of his hand through my shirt. "No, I feel the same way."

I saw Lewis after lunch that day. As predicted, I hadn't been seeing as much of him, now that baseball season had started. The days he'd asked me over to study seemed to be the same days I was seeing Tom. Now, he said, "Hello, stranger."

"Hi." I started to walk on. But he grabbed my hand like he had so many times to stop me running into traffic on U.S. 1.

"Miss you," he said.

"Me too."

"Maybe you can come for dinner tonight?"

"I'll try. I have to go see Mr. Barnes for some extra help in English"

The warning bell rang, and I started to go. Lewis's voice stopped me. "Hey."

I turned.

"You okay?"

"Never better."

When I saw Mr. Barnes at his desk, I knew what I had to do, and I did it.

I kissed him.

He kissed me back, hard, practically eating my lips off, his clumsy hands catching all in my hair. It seemed to last a long time, and at the end, he said, "Oh, God. Oh, God, this is wrong," but I knew he didn't mean it. He just wanted me to disagree with him.

I did. "It's not wrong . . . I love you."

"But you're a kid, a student." He was breathing hard, and I could see the erection through his khakis.

"I'm almost eighteen. I'm almost not a student." I reached over, trailing my fingertips along his thigh. "We just have to be careful a few months."

"A few months." It was almost a wail. "But I love you. I need you."

I kissed him again, long and hard, letting my hands run over him and his over me. He was so pathetic, I should have felt sorry for him. But I didn't feel sorry for him. I didn't feel anything for him.

I said, "We could go to my place. No one's ever home there."

He nodded. It was a turn-on, the power, seeing him surrender everything he knew was right, for me.

When we were doing it, I went somewhere else. I'd learned that with my mom's boyfriend Richard, to take myself out of my body, not feel him inside me, polluting me, not hear him moaning or screaming my name.

When he was finished, he said, "I love you."

I said, "I think you need to leave now. My mother will be home soon."

He nodded, and I handed him his balled-up khakis, slipping his wallet out of the pocket with my other hand, hidden so he couldn't see.

He wanted to kiss me again. I let him. Then I handed him his shirt.

After he left, I didn't shower. I stuck his wallet between the sofa cushions, where she'd be sure to see it. I went next door and knocked on Lewis's door.

I got home early, nine maybe. Mom was holding the wallet.

"Where'd this come from? What you been doing?"

I made my face blank and stared at her. "What is that?"

She slapped me hard across the face. "Don't act all innocent with me." She shoved the wallet at me. "You been stealing?"

I began to cry. My hurting face made it easy. "No...no...you have to believe me. I didn't steal anything."

"Where'd it come from then?"

"It's my English teacher's...Mr. Barnes. He came here. He was going to help me, and he...we..."

Mom didn't look shocked. I remembered what she thought happened with Richard, how she'd blamed me for what he did. "I know how you are with men too...little slut."

I stopped crying and wiped my dry eyes. "It doesn't matter. Even if I consented, even if I *seduced* him..." A laugh at this. "...it's still against the law. I'm a minor, a student." I met Mom's eyes. "People still file lawsuits and get money."

I saw her react to *money*.

An hour later, I was at the police station, telling my story. I hadn't showered. I had all the proof they needed.

I scan the audience, finally finding Lewis near the front with the other *I*'s.

The last time I spoke to him was the day Mr. Barnes left school. Elizabeth left then, too, to live with an aunt or something in some other city. I wasn't really paying attention to where.

Lewis had cornered me at my locker.

"It was him, wasn't it?"

"Hmm?"

"The bet. The one with intrinsic value. It was Mr. Barnes."

I blinked at him. "I have no idea what you're talking about."

"Right."

He started to walk away, but I grabbed his hand. "Hey. I have some time after school. Do you want to go over the word list for the SATs?"

"I don't think I want your help," he said.

After that, every time I saw him, he turned and went the other way.

Now, I clear my throat to finish my speech.

"I stand before you today as your valedictorian because I love a challenge. I haven't had the advantages that some of my classmates have had, but my success is proof that you can accomplish anything...as long as you set your mind to it."

Is the applause scattered? Maybe so. Doesn't matter. I got my scholarship letter last week—a full ride with no stops along the way. Once I walk offstage with my diploma, I can keep right on walking.

Excerpt from Inexcusable

Unfortunately Magnificent

CHRIS LYNCH

I was unfairly famous one time, for a little while. No, I was infamous. No, *notorious.*

Famous, then infamous, then notorious.

Then it all went away and things quieted back down and that's when the shit really started happening.

But the thing is, it was all wrong. It was all unfair and incorrect and ass-backwards. None of it happened the way it should have.

Here's why I got famous. I got famous because I crippled a guy.

He wasn't crippled, exactly, but he surely doesn't play football anymore.

I shouldn't even have been there. That's the thing, understand. I shouldn't even have been there, in that spot, in that game, that day. I don't normally play cornerback, see. I am second-string cornerback. Mostly I'm a kicker. I'm first-string kicker, third-string tight end, and second-string cornerback.

This is significant because of the league we played in. This was not a passing league. This was not a razzle-dazzle league where the ball and the buzz were in the air all the time and there were scouts here from big-time motion-offense colleges like Penn State and Michigan and Florida State looking for talent. This was just another lopey sub-urban league like a million other suburban leagues around the country, full of white wide receivers and built around fullbacks who got their jobs based on the fact that their backs were very full indeed, like the view of a grand piano from above.

So the passing game was not an important thing. Not important to the game, and surely not important to me. Understand, I could have been a starter for this team, as a cornerback, or as a tight end. Coach wanted me to, in fact, always badgered me to play more. But I didn't want to play more. I wanted to play less. Because I was wasting my life at cornerback and tight end. Because I wasn't good. Good enough for this team? Sure. Good enough for any decent college in America? I had a better chance of ice dancing in the Olympics.

Kicker, though, was a different story. There was a reasonable chance I could slip in as a placekicker on a respectable small to midsize program if I worked hard at it.

So I did. And every year I played a little less offense

and defense where I might get mangled, and spent a lot more time on the sidelines kicking the air out of that ball, out of the hands of whoever would hold for me, into that practice net over and over and over.

Until coach dragged me into the game. Other guys needed a breather here and there. And I was no liability on the field, so I had to do my bit when called upon.

Matter of fact, I was an improvement on the guys I replaced. Because I always did what I was told. I always did it by the numbers. I always followed the plan. And I always gave it full-tilt. I wasn't looking for any full-time cornerback job, and I wasn't looking to catch the eye of some division-three scout looking for defensive backs. I was looking to get the job done the way I was taught, and get back to the sidelines where I could kick and remain safe, and get the easiest possible college scholarship so that my dad could come and see me on homecoming day and not have to remortgage the house to pay for the privilege. My dad could come on some excellent homecoming day, my sisters would be up there, Mary on his right and Fran on his left, sitting up there in the sharp, freezing November sun, and then they would be able to see me run onto the field at the end of a big game and *bang* that ball through the posts, just as cool as you like. That would be the moment, wouldn't it? That would be the top. Every eye on me, because the kicker is the only one who can do that, hold every eye, hold the game close to himself, and then Fran and Mary and Dad would be on their feet, screaming louder than everyone, so proud they could just expire, and I would wave dramatically at them, and later we would go to a nice restaurant.

That was my dream. That was as far as my dream went, and I would have stacked my dream up against anyone's.

Which is why I shouldn't have been on the field that day. I should have been working on my field goals because guys were starting to get their offer letters from schools, and I wasn't. I had had some interest, but you would have had to call it tepid if you called it anything. I had to kick.

But first, there was business. It was late in the season, in a game that didn't matter to the state championships or the league standings or even to any of the parents of the players beyond the twelve or so in the stands, but for some reason, the quarterback on the other team started going mental. One of those parents had to be his, and he must have been aware that one or more of the others was a scout with a desperate need for a quarterback and an offer letter in his fist, and that quarterback must have been opening his mail every morning to the same screaming lack of interest from the college football fraternity with time whipping by at whiplash speed.

Because he started to throw. The sonofabitch started to throw. And throw and throw and throw.

I even had to stop kicking to watch. He was immense. He was a monster. I was thinking, jeez, if you had just thrown like this the last three years you could be sitting at home right now comparing illegal incentives from Notre Dame and USC instead of busting your hump trying to get somebody's attention now.

But he sure was kicking the snot out of us. All our defensive players—from our tubbo linemen to our confused concrete linebackers, to our backs who circled and flailed their arms looking like they were flagging down help for one car wreck after another—were absolutely ragged. They had their tongues dragging on the ground as they lamely pursued the quarterback, then when they missed him, the ball, then when they missed that, the receivers. Replacement defenders were shoved onto the field after every play.

Which is how I came to be there, when I shouldn't have been.

I did what I was told. I did what I was taught. I did what I did, what I always did, what I still always do. I followed things to the letter of the law. And I followed things to the spirit of the law.

Football is played to a particularly rough spirit. It's a fact. Some would call it violent. Functioning within that specific world is not the same thing as functioning within the regular one.

They were getting away with a lot of over the middle stuff. Anybody could see that. It's elemental. You cannot just let a team keep throwing the ball right over the middle, behind your linebackers and in front of your corners and safeties, and not make them pay for that. Everybody understands this, and if they don't, then they need to try.

They teach you that from very early on. I learn my lessons. I comprehend the game. I play as I am taught.

Stick 'em.

I saw it unfolding again, the same way I saw it unfolding from the sidelines, play after play, when the guys on the field could probably guess what was happening but were just too whipped to do anything about it. The quarterback took the snap, took three quick long strides back into his pocket, and let sail with a motion too quick practically to even see, more like a baseball catcher throwing out a runner.

The receiver, my guy, my responsibility, was just slanting off his pattern, angling across toward the middle of the field.

You could see it from a mile. There was no decision to be made, really. Autopilot.

I could have closed my eyes and hit him. I mean, right from near the start of the play, I could have shut my eyes tight, and still run full steam, and still arrived at just the right spot at just the right time, me, him, and the ball, because they were doing it so textbook, so simply, so thoughtlessly. It had been too easy. We had made it too easy. They were getting too comfortable. Too lazy, spoiled, entitled. You need to never do that. Never, ever, ever. It is so dangerous out there, you can never ever get spoiled, just because it is coming too easy to you.

When you hit a guy with all your being, hit him the way a car hits a moose, you would expect it to hurt both of you. But it doesn't hurt the hitter, if the hitter has hit perfectly. It is a strange sensation, almost a magical sensation. The car takes a crumpling, and the moose takes a mangling.

But not the hitter. If you do it right, do it the way you have been taught to do it by guys who have smashed into a hundred thousand other guys before and who were taught by guys who had smashed into a hundred thousand other guys.

It's like, you smash right through him. Like he's not even there. Like you go in, you go down, and you just find yourself there, lying as if you are just getting up out of bed. You feel nothing bad. You feel relaxed, even, refreshed. And you do get up, and trot off.

Perfect timing. The defensive back hits the receiver at the instant the ball arrives. A beautiful pop and explosion, like fireworks.

I was already on the sidelines before I knew anything. I was already back, picking up my practice ball, grabbing somebody by the jersey to come hold for me so I could kick a few and make up for lost time. I never received so many hard slaps on the back.

It wasn't a fumble, because he never had a chance to get possession of the ball. It just popped up in the air, straight up, just like the guy's helmet did, and somebody, some straggler from my team who was just standing around waiting to get lucky, got lucky, and caught the ball. Then he fell down, and a lot of other guys fell on top of him.

Great. We were on offense now, and I was off to the sidelines.

Where I became a small-time short-term hero.

"Way to bang him, Keir," somebody said, and banged me on the back.

"Way to stick."

"Mowed him, Keir. Absolutely plowed him right under."

Until it stopped. All of it. Nobody touched me then, nobody said anything more. Some goddamn monster vacuum came and sucked all the sound, all the air and life out of the whole field, as every eye turned to the spot. The spot where I was a few seconds earlier, where I did my job as well as it can be done, where all the coaches were now and all the referees, and several people from up in the stands, and where people were looking back toward the school buildings and waving, waving for even more people to come.

I stood there, all vacuumed out myself, feeling like a head in a helmet floating above where my body should have been.

My holder walked away.

It was news. There were inquiries and investigations and editorials. I was home from school for a week, for my own good, for my peace of mind, because I couldn't possibly concentrate, couldn't hear a word with the constant roar in my ears coming from inside my own head and from all points around it. The phone rang all the time, and my dad answered it. He never put me on the phone, never shied away from a question, never lost his patience with school officials or local radio or whoever. He took off work and stayed there with me and played Risk, the game burning on all week as we took great chunks of continents from one another and then lost them again in between phone calls and lots of silence and lots of talks where he said not much more than that everything was going to work out all right and that it didn't much matter anyway what any investigation said because he already knew, knew me, and knew that his internal, in-his-own-heart investigation had cleared me.

I didn't look at the mail. He did that too. I could tell, though, if he had opened any letters from college football programs. He hadn't. The weird silence again. No acceptances, no rejections the entire week.

By Friday of the week I stayed home, everybody had looked into the accident—that's a funny word, though, isn't it? It was an accident. You know it was an accident. And also, it was no accident, anything but an accident. Everybody concluded—though not happily—that I had not done anything wrong. I had not done anything out of line. I had not done anything blameworthy.

An unfortunately magnificent hit, in the universe of football was what the writer called it, in the article about my being cleared.

The game, Risk, was unchanged at the end of the sorry week. It was right back where we'd started it. In stock-car racing, when there is a wreck on the track, they wave the yellow flag, which means everybody keeps driving, but nobody passes anybody else, nobody changes position, they just continue, motor on, float, high-speed float, until things are stabilized, and you can race again. We ran that week under a yellow flag, me and Dad.

Quietly, I returned to classes the following Monday. Everybody made a great effort to put the incident away, back, in the background, one tackle, late in a game, late in

the season, very late in a high school football life. Very possibly the end of my football life.

When I got home, at the end of that first quiet day, I got the mail, and opened it.

I had quietly received an offer of a football scholarship.

The next day I quietly received two more.

Museum Piece

RON KOERTGE

I don't believe the curator's nonsense
about provenance and the rhythm of shadow
and light, but I love slipping between the
black curtains and watching this grainy
stag movie, the one where somebody
in her underpants can't get any hot water
so she calls a plumber who shows up
in about five seconds.

I saw this the first time when I was fourteen,
working for a dollar an hour plus tips carrying
trays of catfish and cold beer to the Veterans
of Foreign Wars.

It stopped me in my tracks. I gawked as
the Husband came home early and was
at first incensed and then bisexual.

At that the veterans booed and turned
away like bashful virgins in the poems
I'd been reading, the ones that always.
drew a curtain across anything indiscreet.

I couldn't wait to tell my brother, in bed
with a fever, whose place I had taken
at the VFW. I'd give him half the money,
open the beer I'd smuggled out, light the
cigarettes we hid in the garage, and say,
"Goddamn, you won't believe what I just saw!"

About the Contributors

MARTIN MATJE is an acclaimed book illustrator whose work has also appeared in such newspapers as the *Wall Street Journal.* He lives in Canada.

BROCK COLE is a novelist and picture book author and illustrator. His novels include *The Goats* and *The Facts Speak for Themselves,* a National Book Award finalist. He lives in Wisconsin.

JOAN BAUER is an award-winning novelist and short story writer. Her novel *Rules of the Road* won the *Los Angeles Times* Book Prize. She lives in Brooklyn, New York.

NIKKI GRIMES is a poet and novelist. Her novel *Bronx Masquerade* won the 2003 Coretta Scott King Award. She lives in Southern California.

EMMA DONOGHUE is an Irish writer, playwright, and historian. Her novels include *Kissing the Witch* and *The Woman Who Gave Birth to Rabbits.* She lives in Canada.

MARC ARONSON is publisher of Cricket Books and an award-winning author of informational books. His latest book is *Witch-Hunt: Mysteries of the Salem Witch Trials.* He lives in New Jersey.

DAVID PABIAN is a screenwriter. *Leatherstone* is his first novel for young adults. He lives in Los Angeles.

MARK PODWAL is a practicing dermatologist as well as an award-winning artist. His drawings have appeared in the *New York Times* since 1972. He lives in New York.

HAZEL ROCHMAN is former young adult books editor of *Booklist* magazine, the author of *Against Borders,* and coeditor of *Bearing Witness: Stories of the Holocaust.* She lives in Chicago.

TOM FEELINGS was the first African American winner of the Caldecott Honor Medal. His monumental work *The Middle Passage* provides a stunning visual chronicle of the African slave trade.

TERRY DAVIS is the author of the classic young adult novels *Vision Quest* and *If Rock and Roll Were a Machine.* He lives in Minnesota.

SONYA SONES is a poet and photographer. Winner of the Myra Cohn Livingston Award in Poetry, she lives in Santa Monica, California.

GARY MILLER grew up in the oil country of northern Pennsylvania. He studied writing in the Vermont College M.F.A. program and lives in Putnamville, Vermont.

R. GREGORY CHRISTIE is a two-time Coretta Scott King Honor Award winner for illustration. His work has appeared in numerous publications, including the *New Yorker* and *Print.* He lives in Brooklyn, New York.

ELIZABETH LORDE-ROLLINS is a medical doctor and poet. She is the daughter of Audre Lorde. She lives in New York.

ALEX FLINN is an attorney and novelist. Her books include *Breathing Underwater, Breaking Point,* and *Nothing to Lose.* She lives in Florida.

CHRIS LYNCH is the author of a number of acclaimed novels for young adults, including *Freewill,* a Michael L. Printz Honor winner. He lives in Scotland.

RON KOERTGE is a poet and novelist. His books for young adults include *The Arizona Kid* and *Stoner & Spaz.* He teaches in the M.F.A. program at Vermont College and lives in Southern California.

About the Editor

Michael Cart is the author of the young adult novel *My Father's Scar* and editor of a number of award-winning anthologies. Former president of the Young Adult Library Services Association, he teaches young adult literature at UCLA and is the recipient of the 2000 Grolier Foundation Award for his production and promotion of outstanding literature for children and young adults. He appointed and chaired the task force that created the Michael L. Printz Award for excellence in young adult literature. Michael Cart lives in San Diego.